THE ALASTRINE LEGEND

Debbie Nordman

iUniverse LLC
Bloomington

THE ALASTRINE LEGEND

This is a work of fiction. All of the characters, names, incidents, organizations, and dialogue in this novel are either the products of the author's imagination or are used fictitiously.

iUniverse books may be ordered through booksellers or by contacting:

iUniverse LLC
1663 Liberty Drive
Bloomington, IN 47403
www.iuniverse.com
1-800-Authors (1-800-288-4677)

ISBN: 978-1-4917-0492-9 (sc)
ISBN: 978-1-4917-0494-3 (hc)
ISBN: 978-1-4917-0493-6 (ebk)

Library of Congress Control Number: 2013915761

Printed in the United States of America

iUniverse rev. date: 09/23/2013

CONTENTS

CHAPTER 1

Jasper

"WHO ARE YOU AND HOW did you get into my kingdom?" Dwarflord Ganesh Blackstone, king of the dwarves, asked for the second time.

The auburn-haired girl faced the throne. The gathering crowd of dwarves fell silent. All ears tuned to her answer. The huge stone cavern became eerily quiet. "My sister and I were exploring and got lost, okay?" She glanced down at the girl on the floor. "We're sorry we left the designated trails. If you'll let us go, we won't bother you again."

"Explain this 'designated trails' nonsense," the king demanded.

"This is Carlsbad ... Carlsbad Caverns ... the national park, right?"

"No. It's Jasper. Has been for centuries," said Barak, the black-haired dwarf standing next to her.

She shrugged. "Well, in that case, you can forget the 'designated trails' bit."

Barak's eyes narrowed to slits. "You will answer my father's questions without riddles."

"I've told you already. We were exploring when your ruffians kicked us around." She turned to Barak. "You didn't have to be so rough with my sister." She pointed to the girl on the floor, who was now moaning as she slowly came awake.

"You both fought," he said and gestured to the dwarf beside her sister. "We subdued." He folded his arms across his broad chest. "Your names, girl. Your names."

She sighed. "I'm Alison Noland and that"—she pointed—"is my sister, Angela."

———≈≈≈≈———

Inexplicably, the crowd went wild at Angela's name. She tried to rise, feeling quite dizzy. Alison helped her to her feet. The three dwarves closest to them watched with detached curiosity.

At five foot three, Angela Noland felt nervous standing eye-to-eye with many of the dwarves. She had a habit of running her fingers through her hair every time she felt anxious. Therefore, she usually wove the silky stuff into braids that hung to her waist. It needed rebraiding badly now, having come completely loose with the rough treatment she had endured earlier. She glanced over at her twin.

Alison's hair was the same auburn color as Angela's, but it had more curl and it was cut shorter, just reaching her shoulders. Her skin was darker than Angela's, and she was taller by three inches, which made her tower over the dwarves.

Gently touching the back of her head, Angela looked around. She remembered a scuffle. She had been knocked over the head. The three men guarding them were the same ones who had participated in the scuffle. She moaned. If only her head would stop hurting.

In all the current commotion, Angela found no one was paying much attention to her. She took advantage of the private time to reflect upon the people surrounding her. Because of their short, stocky physiques, the dwarves reminded her of dwarves in stories she'd heard as a child. The men had long, forked beards tucked into black breeches. Barak Blackstone, standing beside her and just about her height, had raven-black hair and wore a green tunic under silver-and-black chain mail. A younger version of Barak, wearing similar clothes, stood next to Alison.

The third man, standing behind the girls, had blond hair and a beard. His tunic showed crusty brown under his black-and-brown chain mail. He stood about an inch taller than Barak.

Angela leaned closer to her sister in order to be heard over the chaos. "What's going on? And who is that on the throne?"

Alison nodded in disgust toward the man on the throne. "I've been told his name is Dwarflord Ganesh Blackstone, and I told him our names."

"And that caused this near riot?" Angela replied in astonishment.

"Maybe it was the way I said it?" Alison shrugged.

Angela looked up at the low but vast ceiling. "It looks like we are still in Carlsbad. But who are these people?"

"You got part of that right."

Angela rolled her eyes. "Okay, what do you mean?"

"They call this place Jasper now, not Carlsbad, and I don't know who these people are."

Angela looked closer at her surroundings. "Well, what are your thoughts right now?"

"To be honest, I wish we were someplace else. This place makes me nervous."

Angela took a deep breath. Her sister, nervous? Nothing ever bothered her. Oh, why did she let Alison get them into trouble?

"*Silence!*"

Angela jumped and grabbed Alison's arm. Did that so-called king have to shout like that?

The dwarflord stood and again shouted once more for silence before he was obeyed. "Barak, take these two to my War Room. Then call my captains and counselors for a meeting. We'll take this matter up then."

Barak led the girls through the crowd. Angela used the time to study her surroundings more thoroughly. They were definitely in the Big Room of Carlsbad, although it looked different. The lunchroom was gone and a spiral staircase made of iron replaced the elevators. Several dwarves were climbing the stairs, perhaps to their respective homes, which seemed to be carved into the rock. Whenever one of the many doors lining the cavern walls was opened, she caught glimpses of living areas. If the dwarves carved living spaces from the Big Room walls, wouldn't they do the same elsewhere?

She turned her attention to the people. The men wore chain mail and breeches like Barak's but in different colors. They all wore stout belts, weapons hanging from some, and tools from others. The weapons consisted of double-bitted axes and knives. The tools were ordinary hammers and chisels of all sizes—tools used to work stone.

The women in the caverns wore long, flowing robes of a white material tied with colorful beaded ropes about their waists. Each woman had braided her hair with beads and ribbons to match the ropes. Some of them had piled the braids on top of their heads like tiaras while others allowed theirs to hang to their waists.

The children wandering around were dressed similarly to the women with one exception: their robes were colorful and their belts were either black or white. The younger ones laughed and played, running here and there. The older ones tended fires and helped the women regardless of gender. Angela watched as several youngsters stopped their work and stared at them before the adults nearby regained their attention.

Torches and sconces hung along the walls, emitting an amber glow that lighted the caverns. With all the fires, she was surprised no smoke hung in the air. The floors felt smoother than she remembered too. With all the changes, she could only guess at what events might have occurred after they found themselves lost and then were suddenly knocked out.

Why had she let Alison talk her into exploring? They should have stayed on the marked trail. Alison had made it sound so exciting. And she'd insisted that, if they left their earphones near the passage they took, a park ranger would be able to find them if they got lost and failed to return to the entrance before closing time. Well, they got lost, and with Alison's persistence, they wandered for hours. When no help came and their flashlights dimmed, Angela insisted they stop and wait. They had barely settled in, leaning against the cavern wall, when their flashlights gave out. As they sat in total darkness and an eerie silence, time passed slowly, broken only by the hollow, watery sound of an occasional drip from far off.

Hours later, a bright light blinded them. Angela recalled becoming extremely nauseated before sliding into unconsciousness. When she awoke, Alison was arguing with three short, stocky men. She tried to break up the fight only to be knocked out. Her next thought occurred when she woke up surrounded by the crowd in the Big Room and found herself guarded by the same three men.

What happened to us? Why is Carlsbad now called Jasper and occupied by "dwarves"? I must be dreaming. None of this makes sense. This can't be real! She shook her head thinking it would clear her thoughts. Nothing changed.

Barak opened a door. He ushered them inside and closed the door, leaving them alone.

Angela sat down in one of the ten chairs around the oval table that took up most of the space in the room. "Now," she began, "tell me what happened after I got knocked out." She concentrated on her hair, getting it back into its braids and out of her eyes, while Alison explained.

"They overpowered me when you were knocked out. Two held me captive while Barak—"

"The one who escorted us in here?"

"Yes. He picked you up. They took us to that circus we just left." Alison sat down. "I don't know how we ended up here. We sure aren't where we were."

Angela rose and went to a big map occupying one wall. She ignored the weapons hanging on the other three walls. "Well, at least we aren't lost anymore. This is definitely Carlsbad, though they call it Jasper. This sounds crazy, but maybe we're in an alternate dimension."

"Yeah, that sounds crazy." Alison scoffed and rolled her eyes. She rose and walked to the nearest wall of weapons. "Wherever we may be, I'm impressed with what I see here."

Angela smiled. Her sister sure loved to examine weapons of all sorts. Turning back to the map she was studying, she called out. "Alison, what do you make of this mark near our home?" She pointed to Ozark country.

Joining her twin, Alison studied the map a moment. "It seems to resemble Greek lettering."

"I thought so too. This looks like part of the symbol for alpha, while this looks somewhat like omega, the last letter."

Alison agreed. Leaning around Angela, she said, "Here's the same symbol over the Grand Canyon. I wonder what it means."

At that moment, Dwarflord Ganesh entered the War Room and took a seat at the table directly opposite the only door in or out of the room. His sons entered next. Barak led the girls to the table and pulled out two chairs for them. After making sure they were comfortable, he took a seat on their left between Angela and the dwarflord. *Well,* Angela thought, *he's more courteous now than he was before.*

More dwarves filed in. One of the two dwarves who had aided in their capture sat on the girls' right. The other, a blond-bearded dwarf, sat opposite Barak. The chamber filled quickly with three of the four remaining seats being taken. A low murmur permeated the air. Angela heard the words *Alastrine Legend* and *Ahriman* repeatedly. At least the dwarves were quieter than they'd been earlier.

A man strolling toward the remaining seat opposite Angela caught her eye. She'd never seen such an attractive and unusual creature before. He was taller than the dwarves, and his ears and brows swept upward. His silvery-blond hair hung to his shoulders. He was physically fit with a long, well-proportioned body. Dressed in a light-brown tunic and breeches, he carried no weapon she could see. She thought that unusual, since every male in these caverns seemed to, if they weren't carrying tools.

Barak reached over the table and shook hands with the pointed-eared stranger. "Avery, my good elf, what brings you to Jasper?"

Avery smiled. "The Alastrine Legend." His soft voice, touched with a hint of huskiness, fit the man.

He glanced at Angela. Her heart fluttered. *What beautiful cobalt-blue eyes,* she thought. They were almost iridescent. His eyes bored into her misty-blue ones. She felt stripped of her defenses. Was he reading her mind?

Avery broke eye contact when Dwarflord Ganesh rose. Angela took a deep breath, realizing she had been holding it. *What is wrong with me? A strange being stares at me and I turn from being a woman of seventeen years to a giddy schoolgirl. Chill!* she told herself.

The room grew quiet. All eyes turned to the dwarflord. He looked over the assembly. "We have a very important decision to make," he began, then smiled. "Yes, Hadek?"

"Sire, has the Alastrine Legend come to life?" A scraggly red-bearded dwarf pointed at the girls. He appeared very young.

"I don't know. That is one of the questions needing answers."

"Their names sound similar to the ones in the legend," said another dwarf. Heads bobbed in agreement.

A third dwarf gestured at the girls. "Neither looks stout enough to destroy Ahriman. Why should we think either is the one?"

Barak stood. "Because we three"—he pointed to himself and the two others as he said their names—"Devlak, Telek, and I found them in the South Passage. No one saw them until we happened upon them. There is no way anyone could get into that particular passage without being seen. They would have been noticed immediately." He sat down. Murmurs of agreement rose from the others.

At last, Angela knew her captors' names. Devlak looked like a younger version of Barak, possibly a brother. The blond-bearded dwarf was Telek.

"I need more proof than that, Barak," said a white-haired dwarf sitting directly opposite Dwarflord Ganesh. "What were you three doing in that particular passage, anyway?"

"Mandek, my old friend, what my sons do for me is of no concern to anyone but me. All that matters is that they were in that passage and found these girls. Before we have any more questions, let's see what our elfin friend has to say."

Avery stood and bowed to Ganesh. "We are at the crossroads spoken of so many years ago. I've been sent to bring back the Alastrine Savior. Queen Kalika informed me she is here." He turned his attention to Angela and looked into her eyes for a moment before continuing. "My Lord, only the queen can tell us if one of these two girls is the one we're looking for." He sat down as several dwarves argued.

Angela glanced around. Why had that elf looked at her before mentioning a savior? Surely he didn't think she was this "savior." She traded looks with her twin.

Alison stood. In a commanding voice, she exclaimed, "Excuse me!" With everyone's attention focused upon her, she continued, "Explain this 'Alastrine Savior' bit. The way you all are reacting, we think it has something to do with us. I demand we both be told what it is." She sat down and smiled at Angela, who nodded in agreement.

Dwarflord Ganesh glared at Alison. He didn't like her making demands. *Too bad*, Angela thought.

He seemed to make up his mind and started to speak. "The Alastrine Legend has been passed down from generation to generation. It tells of a woman savior who will be sent to destroy Evil before Evil destroys the world. When or how this is accomplished is not known. The signs to look for were never told either. We only know that the Dwarven Nation will set eyes upon her first, while the Elfin Nation will verify her identity. Your unusual presence and Avery's appearance are enough to cause our suspicions."

"What is this 'evil'?" asked Angela. "And how is it supposed to destroy the world?"

Barak's voice sounded deeper than before. "According to the legend, Evil will bring plagues to all living things, even the plants."

"He will make the world a desolate vastness where nothing survives," added Devlak, sitting next to Alison.

"There is only one clue to her identity," said the dwarflord. "She will be homeless, with no land to call her own."

Angela Noland's heart skipped a beat and then began to beat hard and fast. She desperately wanted to flee, but too many dwarves stood between her and the door. This had to be a nightmare. If she would only wake up, all would be fine.

"Did the legend describe this savior at all?" Alison asked.

"No." Avery turned to the head of the table. "My Lord, may I inquire as to the names of these two?" Everyone followed his gesture toward the girls.

Dwarflord Ganesh stared at them, eyebrows raised.

Alison glared back. "Fine," she said. She stood once again. "I am Alison." She sat back down. "Your turn," she whispered to Angela.

Slowly, Angela stood, holding on to the table. The room became deathly quiet. With wobbly legs she stared at the tabletop and said, "My name is … Angela Noland." Slowly, she sat back down. With sudden courage she raised her head high and stared at Avery, daring him to say she was the one he had come for.

Calmly, he looked back. After a moment, he turned to Dwarflord Ganesh. "Sire, I ask for your permission to take the girls back to Krikor with me. For as I said earlier, Queen Kalika can tell us if one is indeed the Savior. Only then can we all know the truth and be assured she is here."

The dwarflord nodded. "Does anyone disagree?" No one spoke. "It is settled. When will you leave, Avery? And how many men do you wish to accompany you?"

"Wait a minute," Angela interrupted, her courage still with her. The dwarflord glared at her interference. "Things are moving too fast for us. We have no idea where we are, and you people are talking about us as if we aren't here. I don't like that. I know my sister doesn't either."

"She's right," Alison added. "Who is Queen Kalika and what is Krikor?"

"My liege and my home," Avery stated. "If you are who we think, we will train you for your destiny."

Alison crossed her arms. "I don't think so. I am not happy about being here, and neither my sister nor I will go anywhere. We need more information than that."

"We believe one of you will determine the fate of this world. In order to do that, I need to take you to Krikor."

"As I said before," argued Alison, "I don't wish to go anywhere and neither does Angela."

Angela chuckled at her sister's stubbornness.

Avery studied each girl in turn and then said, "Sire, I will send one of my men to go back to Krikor and let the queen know what has transpired here. I would like to remain. If you agree, the girls will stay in your custody until he returns."

Dwarflord Ganesh nodded. "Does that suit you and your sister?" he asked Alison.

She smiled her agreement.

"Okay. While we wait, Avery, I plan to have my sons begin training the girls. Perhaps that will prove to make them more agreeable to things here in the months to come." He sighed when, once again, Alison interrupted him.

"What training are you talking about?"

Barak laughed. "Father, her stubbornness is a trait we need." He turned to answer Alison. "I will train you both in fencing. It is a skill that may save your lives."

"I shall train you in archery," Avery added. "It is a good idea to have more than one skill to fall back on." His eyebrows raised, he looked toward the dwarflord for confirmation.

"Sounds good to me." Dwarflord Ganesh smiled. "I will have Serylda teach them about the world we live in today."

"Fine," Alison agreed. "I hate to be idle, and it seems to me we'll be here a while. Now, one more question. Who is Serylda?"

"My daughter, who is as stubborn as you."

Angela's brows knitted together. "I'm not comfortable about the implication that our lives may be in danger. Why do we have to learn fencing and archery?"

"They are just skills we will teach you." Barak crossed his arms. "Odds are you won't need them."

Angela glanced down at her clasped hands and hoped he was right.

Ignoring the girls, Dwarflord Ganesh Blackstone rose to address the assemblage. "It seems we will have visitors for a few months. I charge everyone to make them feel at home. My family will give the girls room and board. I expect no trouble. Pass my instructions on to every dwarf in the kingdom. Dismissed." A rousing cheer burst forth from every throat in the chamber, reverberating throughout the room and beyond. One of the dwarves thrust the door open, and the dwarves began to file out. After exchanging a few words with Barak, Devlak approached the girls.

"If you two will follow me, I'll take you to refreshments and perhaps a nap." He led them out of the War Room and back into the Big Room.

"How many people live here?" Angela asked, looking around. The caverns were alive with busy dwarves of all sizes.

"At the present time, I think we have around eight hundred fifty men, women, and children living in Jasper. We also have clans in Boman, the ancient cavern system near Krikor. We will teach you about this and more."

Angela concentrated on listening to Devlak. His voice, not as harsh or as low pitched as Barak's, was a comfort nonetheless. She still felt too apprehensive to relax. She knew Alison had an easier time adjusting to new situations. She willed herself to remain calm and hoped answers would come to her questions before long. *It can't be soon enough*, she thought.

Devlak stopped in the center of the Big Room, his arms spread wide in a gesture that included the entire cave. "Ages ago, according to our histories," he began, "before the Great Catastrophe, people came here to relax. Our ancestors escaped into these and other cavern systems to survive with the aid of the Ancient Ones. Over there"—he pointed—"was a lunchroom of sorts. Now, it serves as a public gathering place. And there—" He pointed at the spiral staircase.

"Were elevators," Angela interrupted. "Yes, we know. We called this place Carlsbad."

Devlak turned his attention to Alison. "Hey, that's what *you* called Jasper." He chuckled. "Well, as I was about to say, our ancestors made living quarters in the walls of the shaft as we needed the room." He stopped walking and smiled at both girls. "I realize all this sounds strange. I understand more than most. I have a tendency to want answers immediately also. Please be patient."

The girls nodded, and Devlak led them into a short passage that ended at a door. The passage looked man-made. He opened the door and called for his mother. A young woman appeared.

"Hello, brother. Mother is busy." She wiped her hands on her apron. She had the same dark hair as Devlak. But instead of it being braided, it hung loose, reaching her waist.

"Serylda, make these girls at home. Father has decided they are to stay with us for a few months. They can stay in the guest quarters." He turned to the girls. "My sister will take care of you."

He left as Serylda led them back out into the passage and next door into another room. "You two must be the reason everyone's talking about the Alastrine Legend." Her voice carried soft and soothing undertones. They felt very welcomed for it. She led them to the couch before leaving, saying she'd have refreshments sent shortly.

"Well, Alison. What are you thinking now?" Angela looked over the cozy room.

Alison sat down. "I wonder what happened to the Earth to radically change it like this."

"Yes. It's hard to believe we're surrounded by dwarves and other faeries."

Alison glared at her twin, her left eyebrow arched. "Excuse me? Your 'books' are showing again."

Angela smiled and shrugged. She sat down next to Alison. "Did you see how that elf stared at me? Avery, I think was his name. It was eerie to say the least."

"What do you mean?" Alison's eye narrowed.

"Oh, I don't know. It was like … well, he held me spellbound. I couldn't look away."

"He was looking at me, sis," Alison said. She leaned back and closed her eyes. "He's mine. So stay away from him."

Angela shook her head at her sister's annoying ways. Another male would soon find himself in Alison's sights.

A boy entered carrying a tray of food—various fruits, crackers, and cheeses. Behind him came a young girl with a tray that held two goblets of a fruity-looking beverage. They set their trays down on a small table near the door, and with a bow, left. After devouring the contents of both the trays, the girls returned to the couch. The beverage had been slightly alcoholic, and Alison fell asleep in moments. Angela envied her sister's ability to do that anywhere. She, on the other hand, despite the calming drink, was far from sleep and tried to not worry about their circumstances.

To take her mind off their situation, she decided now would be a good time to do something with her hair again. She used her fingers like a comb. It took her a little time to braid the silky stuff. She always kept it braided, as it was easier to control. She thought once again about cutting it, but dismissed that thought as she usually did. She leaned back and closed her eyes. *So much has happened.* She felt drained now that she allowed herself to relax. Maybe a nap would be good. She chuckled. Perhaps she'd wake up and this really would all be a dream …

Barak and Avery entered the room, waking the girls. *So far,* Angela thought, *it's real.*

"I will take you to our training area," Barak began. "We will show you a few of the things you will need to learn in order to survive in our time."

The months that followed rushed by. The girls trained hard and learned all they could of their new world. Angela showed an aptitude for archery, while Alison appeared to excel with the sword. Some things, however, were left for another time. The Alastrine Legend remained a mystery to them. The excuse Dwarflord Ganesh gave them for not enlightening them was that he believed the girls weren't ready for the real reason they found themselves a few thousand years in the future. And no one could tell them how they'd arrived in a future different from their own. This frustrated Angela the most. In this, she learned how stubborn dwarves could be.

Serylda taught them about the dwarves in general. They learned that dwarves were descended from a working class of the Ancient Ones, but Serylda was reluctant to expand upon just who these Ancient Ones were. "Besides," Serylda explained, "keeping you uninformed about some things will teach you patience."

Angela had an easier time with that concept than did Alison. Even so, some things remained the same, Alison's jealousy of Angela being one of them. One day, Avery worked with the girls on their archery skills. Alison got annoyed when Avery praised Angela on her ability to handle herself. After practice she confronted Angela in their sitting room. "Why do you always have to be the best?" Alison began.

"Please don't start that, Alison. I can't help it if you have a harder time grasping things."

"It's just like back home. You got the better grades. You got the boys." Alison slumped down on the couch. "I hoped it would be different here."

"Okay," Angela joined her, "what is the real problem?"

"I love Avery. I told him so, and he said I didn't know what I was saying."

Angela sighed. She couldn't be annoyed with Alison. She felt something for the elf as well. "That makes you mad at me?"

"Well, he said I should act like you. That I was too impetuous. What's that supposed to mean?"

"It means, dear sister, you have the tendency to jump when you shouldn't. You want things done immediately instead of waiting for the right time."

"Yeah, that's me." And with those words Alison stormed into the bedroom.

Angela rose. She groaned and followed her sister. Tomorrow Barak had said he would decide if they were battle ready.

CHAPTER 2

D WARFLORD GANESH BLACKSTONE ORDERED A meeting in the War Room the next day. They sat as they had when the girls had found themselves in the room the first time. Avery asked to address the assembly first. The dwarflord nodded his agreement.

Avery rose. "Sire, I've received word from Queen Kalika. She is ready to test the girls. She believes they have remained sequestered long enough. It is time for them to see this world."

"Are we going to see the damage from the world war?" Angela asked.

"Perhaps on our journey to Krikor you'll get the chance to see the ruins of some of the major cities," Avery said as he sat down. "We won't get too close, though. They are hazardous places, both in terms of radiation and people who've adapted to them, as you have learned."

"It'll be good to see more than this cave," said Alison. "I've been looking forward to seeing some of the destruction caused by the Great Catastrophe Serylda taught us about. And, yes," she said, rolling her eyes, "you don't have to remind me again, Avery. I know it's dangerous."

Dwarflord Ganesh raised his brows at Avery. "Before you take them to Krikor," he said, turning his attention to his firstborn sitting to his right, "I want Barak to test them."

"Yes, Father." Barak bowed his head. "I plan to do that outside. I'm sending Hadek to gather what I need for the test when this meeting is over."

"Good." Dwarflord Ganesh nodded. He took a deep breath and changed the subject. "Now, Avery, when do you wish to leave? How many of my warriors would you like to accompany you?"

"I'll let you decide that, Sire. But the sooner we leave the better. As you know, it'll take between five and six weeks to reach Krikor. And Ahriman has troops combing the countryside. The Elfin Nation now believes he knows the Savior is here and is looking for her, too." He paused, looked at Angela a moment, and then returned his attention back to the dwarflord. "There is something else you need to know before you make your decision," he said gravely. "Ahriman is planning some new evil for the world. He wants all the free nations to bow down before him or he will use some sort of new weapon. We have no idea what this weapon is. Be warned, it may spell the end of the world. I wish I could tell you more. We have emissaries out trying to learn more about this new evil."

"Thank you, Avery." Dwarflord Ganesh lowered his head and thought for a moment. All eyes watched him, and a murmur permeated the room. He raised his head and the room grew quiet once more. "As I am the dwarflord, it is imperative that I stay here," he said. "And with the threat of war on our doorstep, I cannot send an army with you." He turned to his sons. "Barak, take twenty men and what provisions you'll need. Since you'll be able to find food along the way, I suggest packing lightly to be ready for anything. One other thing, take Devlak with you. He needs the experience." Devlak smiled at his father. Everyone stood when Dwarflord Ganesh stood. "This meeting is adjourned. Good luck, my sons." The dwarflord raised his voice. "The dwarves of Jasper salute you in your quest!"

A rousing cheer followed everyone out of the room. Barak laid a hand on Angela's arm. "Please, I want you and your sister to go to my home and await me there. I will send someone to get you when I am ready. He will have all your provisions with him."

Both girls nodded their understanding and left. Angela looked forward to seeing Serylda one more time. She still owed Serylda a thank-you for the clothes Alison and she now wore. They looked just like all the dwarf females now, with white robes and their own beaded belts. If all went well, she felt they would be on the way to Krikor after Barak tested them.

At the Blackstones' door, Angela knocked. Dwarflady Galinia answered. "If you're looking for Serylda, she said she had something to do," she informed the girls. "She asked me to apologize for her if you showed up here. I'll have refreshments brought to you in the sitting room if you'd like to wait there."

Angela, a bit disappointed, agreed, and they followed her into the sitting room. They waited for an hour after dining on fruit and cheese with a light wine. Still no Serylda. Alison laid her head back and fell asleep almost immediately.

Angela chuckled. *Figures,* she thought. *The same old Alison.* And that was her last thought before she fell asleep too.

Barak entered the room, waking the girls. "It's time to leave," he said, handing each of the girls breeches, a tunic, and a silky cape. He ordered them to change clothes, turned, and left.

Angela, roused from her unexpected but welcomed nap, felt better and looked around. Serylda was still missing. *Oh, well.*

The girls replaced the robes they wore with the breeches and tunics Barak had supplied. They looked like the men now, ready for anything, minus the chain mail. They opened the door and found Barak in the hall waiting for them.

"I thought you were sending someone else to get us," Alison interjected as she shook the folds out of her cape. Barak glared at her as Angela began to look at her cape.

Taking Barak's attention off her sister, Angela asked, "Is there any way we can thank your mother and sister for their hospitality?"

"If either one of you is indeed the Savior, then it is we who should thank you for gracing our home," Devlak answered for Barak as he arrived with three packs in his arms. He handed one to each girl and kept the third for himself.

Barak ushered them out of the room and closed the door. "Yes, but first we need to make sure, and we can't accomplish that standing around here."

He led them to the Gathering Room, also known as the Big Room. No one noticed the small dwarf stealthily following. A small group of twenty men stood waiting near the spiral staircase. Angela recognized blond-haired Telek standing among them. She had recognized a family resemblance in Devlak and Barak, even in Serylda. Though he had blond hair, Telek had similar features. Was he another sibling? She had meant to ask Serylda the next time she saw her. She would just have to ask Telek himself now.

The group began a forced march, not up the staircase but farther into the caverns, an area the girls hadn't been allowed in before. One more dwarf secretly joined the company. Shortly, Angela noticed the walls looked hand carved. They weren't following the natural way to the surface. These ingenious people must have carved a way to the valley below. The trek to the outside, albeit along a different route from the one they'd used when they'd entered the cavern, had begun.

Outside the air was cool and dry, a typical early spring morning in the desert. It was the tenth of March, if Angela hadn't lost count. *I'll ask Devlak later*, she thought as she looked around. They were in the valley below the natural entrance. From their position, no one could know a cavern system existed. All she saw were cacti everywhere, not even a sign of modern industry—no airplanes in the sky, no vehicles anywhere. In fact, the one road she saw was a dirt path.

Behind her stood the Guadalupe Mountains. At least some things still looked the same. She recalled the times she and Alison had hiked to the top of El Capitan of the Guadalupe Mountains, the highest point in Texas. *Well*, she corrected herself, *there may no longer be a "Texas" or "New Mexico." Who knows what these areas are called now?* Serylda had never mentioned anything about it.

The company milled about, waiting for everyone to exit the caverns. When Barak and Avery arrived, all eyes turned toward them for instructions. Avery glanced over at Angela. When he smiled and winked, Angela's legs threatened to give out beneath her.

Avery looked more handsome than ever to her. A cape hung from his shoulders, nearly touching the ground. The color of the material mimicked the surroundings, shimmering in gold, browns, and greens as he moved, giving him a mysterious quality.

Why had she allowed herself to fall for him? Granted he had trained the girls in archery, and Alison had made a fool of herself at one point when she'd thrown herself at him. But that was a month ago. Angela had to forget her feelings for Avery. She hoped Alison would behave too. They weren't elves.

Angela checked the cape draped over her left arm. It shimmered like Avery's and felt silky to the touch. Had he supplied the capes? She wished she had a hat too. The sun was getting hot despite the fact it was only early March. She watched Avery come toward them. Had he just read her mind? Her heart beat faster with each step he took. Why did he affect her like that?

He smiled. "The desert sun can be most unforgiving." He showed her the hood folded inside the cape. "The cape will shade you from the harshness of the sun. I suggest you both put them on while you wait to be tested. They are made to keep you cool in summer and warm in winter. My people made them."

"Thanks." Alison beamed and accepted his advice.

Suddenly too nervous to say a word, Angela just nodded and smiled. But Avery didn't let her get away with that. He stood there, not moving, just smiling at her. Angela found the nerve to say thanks, and he walked off to join Barak.

With his black hair, full beard, and steel helmet, Barak stood like a Viking ready for war. *I'm glad I'm not his enemy*, Angela thought as she donned the cape. Even so, she felt his confidence from where she stood.

He gestured for the girls to join him. "It is time for your tests," he announced. "Hadek, please give me the weapons I asked you to obtain."

Hadek handed three swords and a bow with a quiver of arrows to Barak and stepped back to join the others. While Barak readied his tests, everyone settled down. Most of the soldiers sat down in the shade of a rock outcropping nearby. A few wandered around.

Barak ordered two men to set up a target fifty paces away. Angela was awarded the privilege of beginning this test. He handed her the bow and only one arrow.

She took the weapon and tried to smile. "Don't I get a practice shot first?"

He shrugged and backed off. She sighed.

She strung the bow, nocked the arrow onto the string, pulled the string back, took aim, and let loose the arrow. It passed to the left of the target and imbedded itself in the sand. She closed her eyes. That was bad ... very bad. She had done better the first time she'd held a bow back in her old life.

Barak stared at her. She sighed again. She didn't really know why they had to take these silly tests. But she had to show them she was good enough to "defend" herself even though they weren't going into battle—they were going to Krikor.

With sudden courage, she marched back to Barak and took two arrows from the quiver at his feet. She returned to her starting point and laid the arrows on the ground in front of her. Kneeling on one knee, she nocked an arrow onto the string. Taking a deep breath, she pulled the string taut and let loose the arrow. Before it hit the target, she had the second arrow nocked and loosed. Both hit the target near dead center. She exhaled and rose. Thank the heavens she'd retained the skill Avery had instilled in her.

A cheer went up from the watching dwarves. Angela smiled and then faced Barak. She jutted her chin out as far as she could make it.

He smiled. "I'll grant you that first practice shot." He looked back at the target. "You're good. You had me fooled at first. I'd like to see you and Avery in a contest. I bet it'd be close."

Angela's heart skipped a beat when Avery's name was spoken. She willed her heart to calm down. She didn't want to jump every time she heard the name *Avery*. That would make for a long trek.

"Your turn," Barak said to Alison. He picked up two of the swords. They were made of strong, light wood—the practice swords the girls had been using for weeks! Angela wondered why Hadek had brought out two practice swords along with a real one.

"What's this?" Alison laughed and held up one of the practice swords.

"No one is to get hurt. Don't worry. These are stout enough for my test."

Without warning Barak raised his sword and rushed Alison. Her response was immediate, her wooden sword coming up to parry his thrust.

Angela watched intently. Barak held nothing back. He pressed Alison with his skill and superior strength. She retreated, keeping her balance. Her performance showed her persistence. She kept retreating and parrying Barak's blows. Angela saw the confidence Devlak had helped Alison develop when Barak hadn't been teaching her.

A few of the watching dwarves had to move out of the way as Barak kept up the pressure, backing Alison into the observers. She kept her concentration on Barak. The fight lasted five long minutes, and then Barak made his move. Alison's sword went flying. Without missing a beat, she somersaulted and retrieved her sword in time to counter his final thrust. Surprise showed in his face, and he backed off. The test ended.

"Well done," he said, bowing. She bowed back, wiping sweat from her forehead and hair from her face. He was breathing normally while she panted from the exercise. Retrieving the real sword, Barak exchanged it for the wooden one in Alison's hand. He threw her wooden sword and his own toward the outcropping, barely missing his men standing nearby.

She took the weapon from its scabbard and checked its edge, turning the blade to and fro. "Whose sword is this? It's a fine work of art. Very well made."

"Mine," said Barak, smiling. "I was taught with it as a child. Keep it. My gift to you for learning how to wield such a weapon correctly."

"Thanks." She sheathed the sword and strapped it onto her side. "Tell me, why give me something so valuable?"

"You've earned it. You paid attention to my instruction well."

"Is the bow yours, too?" Angela asked.

Avery walked up behind her. "The bow was mine. I gave it to Barak as a sign of our deep friendship. And, like Barak, I approve of him giving this weapon to you, Angela. It will serve you well." He turned to Barak. "I have an extra knife with me. I propose Angela should have it. As we both know, there are times when a bow is ineffective. And that is when a warrior has to fight hand-to-hand combat."

"Wait," Angela interrupted. Her heart skipped a beat. "Am I going to have to kill someone? I'm not a warrior. I can't do that. Here," she said. She tried to give the bow back to Barak, but he refused it. "I really thought I'd be hunting for food." Her arm dropped to her side, but she still hung on to the weapon.

"We hope you don't have to kill," said Avery. "But if you have to, you need to know how. I'll teach you what you'll need to know." Patting her on the shoulder, he added, "We'll try to keep you safe."

He handed her the knife encased in its own sheath and walked off, retrieving his pack. Gingerly she looked at it. Battle was becoming too real a prospect to Angela. She prayed he was right, that she'd have no reason to use these things or have to kill a living being.

She looked over at her sister. Alison appeared more confident about the prospect of killing. *Please, dear sister*, Angela thought, *don't think this is a game.* The sheathed knife felt heavy in her hand. *It's becoming too real for both of us.*

"I want you two to walk behind Avery and me." Barak's voice broke into her musings. "The rest of my army will follow."

"Is that to keep us safe?" Alison asked.

"Everyone to your feet!" Barak yelled, ignoring her. "Time to go." He retrieved his own pack from the pile near the cavern entrance.

A rather small dwarf handed Angela the three arrows she had shot. She thanked him and replaced them in her quiver. She strapped the weapons onto her back and slung the pack onto her shoulders, still wondering what was in it. She joined Alison behind Avery and Barak, and the march to Krikor began in earnest.

"Angela, have you checked out our weapons? I mean really looked them over?"

"Well, not really, no. Why?"

"I recognize them. They came from the War Room, from that wall of weapons I admired."

Angela frowned. "You're taking this whole 'killing' thing too easily, sister."

Alison smiled and shrugged. "So? You're too soft. What about the weapons?"

Angela shook her head at her sister. "You're too cavalier. Besides, why would they give us those? They looked like a special collection, like they were in a kind of museum on that wall. I think I'll ask Barak or Avery about them." She smiled but started to frown again. Alison glared at her. "What's wrong now?"

"You. I told you before, Avery is mine." Alison faced forward and began a rigid march.

"You're acting jealous." Angela's frown grew deeper. "Please don't do something stupid. Avery is no one's property."

Alison scoffed. "You're always afraid I'll do something stupid. Anyway, he's going to teach you how to fight with a knife. Isn't that enough? Do you have to talk to him, also?"

Angela looked skyward and sighed. "You're crazy. I really don't want to learn how to kill someone. And I can't believe you would either. You know that. But just because Avery is going to teach me something and I thought to ask him a question, you act resentful." She shook her head. "There are times I don't understand you. I'm finding somebody else to talk to. Someone who isn't mad at me. See you later, sis."

Angela slowed down, letting Alison pass ahead of her. Angela was disobeying Barak by not staying directly behind him. She couldn't help it. She wasn't putting up with Alison's madness. That sister of hers got so uptight at the smallest things and pouted for hours. When Alison was in one of her moods, it was difficult to be around her.

Directly behind Angela walked scraggly-bearded Hadek, the company's cook, and Telek, who smiled and nodded. She didn't feel like talking to either one. She smiled back and bent down to pick up a rock, allowing the men to pass her.

Angela's thoughts were a jumble. How in the world had she and Alison ended up here? And in this time? Wasn't this impossible? *It's going to take forever to get to Krikor,* she mused, *but that's where I'll get my answers.*

Someone nearly ran into her before he caught himself. He didn't excuse himself. He just glanced at her, and then, just as quickly, glanced away. He was the small dwarf who had handed her those arrows. The same small dwarf who had followed them out of Jasper.

His black hair reminded Angela of Barak. Was this yet another brother? Maybe one who was supposed to stay at home? How many brothers did Barak have? Maybe this dwarf would talk to her. She hurried to catch up to him. "Hello," she said. "Would you care for some company? I know I would."

The dwarf looked her way before turning his attention back to the trail. He didn't even smile. *Well, that didn't work!* Angela glanced at the clouds overhead trying to think of something else to say. "We might be in for some rather hot weather. What do you think?" *That's a safe topic,* she thought.

The dwarf shrugged, still not saying a word.

"Are you related to Barak by any chance?" *Maybe that will get him talking.* "You resemble him, I think."

The dwarf stared hard at her, a startled look on his face. *That got his attention.* He looked ahead, seeming to contemplate, but not saying a word.

"Well, I guess I'll leave you alone," she said. "Sorry to have bothered you."

Angela slowed down again. But, so did the dwarf. *Interesting.* Was he just shy or was Angela right in thinking he was a brother disobeying the dwarflord? She would play his game. She stooped and picked up another rock. It worked again. Only two dwarves remained behind them. Several paces back strode the rear guards.

"Is this more to your liking?" she asked the dwarf, keeping her voice low.

"Yes, much. Thanks," he said. His voice sounded suspiciously feminine. "Before you say anything, I want you to promise you won't give me away. I know you recognize my voice."

That dwarf was right. Angela knew Serylda's voice after all the things she had taught the twins. What was she doing here? And what happened to her beautiful, long hair?

"Hi." Serylda smiled before becoming serious. "Please don't let Barak—or anyone for that matter—know I'm here. I knew the moment I talked you'd know who I was."

"Serylda, why are you taking this chance?" Angela shook her head. "I can't believe you didn't stay home away from danger."

"I had to come. My lifelong dream was to someday meet the Alastrine Savior. And, if I did, to go with her to help defeat Ahriman. I've prepared all my life." Serylda stopped and laid a hand on Angela's arm. "I believe you are she. So, I cut my hair and followed. Promise me you won't give me away. Barak would send me back. I won't go back. I'll just follow you."

Angela smiled and thought a moment. "Okay. For a favor."

Serylda's hand dropped. She looked apprehensive but determined. "I will not go back. Don't ask me that."

"Don't worry." Angela chuckled. "Just be my friend. Alison is in one of her hard-to-get-along-with moods. I know she does that when she's not sure of herself. But I don't feel like putting up with her at the moment. As it is, I'm not too sure of myself."

Serylda let out a deep sigh of relief. "It's a deal. Maybe I can help you gain some confidence. But call me *Darik* around others. It's an old family name."

"Agreed, Darik. However, you have another problem that name won't solve. Your voice will give you away."

"Some of our people have taken a vow of silence for various reasons, mostly for religion. I'll use that for an excuse."

"Like you're contemplating the future and our success. But, you're talking to me. Doesn't that break your vow?"

"You're the Alastrine Savior. That makes it okay if I talk to you or Alison."

"I still have a problem with that 'Alastrine Savior' bit," Angela said.

"In what way?"

"I wasn't anticipating having to kill anyone. Now I've been given a bow and a knife. That's a little unnerving. And I still don't know what the Alastrine Legend is supposed to be."

"I'm sorry everyone is keeping that a secret. Perhaps at camp tonight you should bring it up."

Angela thanked her for her suggestion.

Serylda was quiet for a second. "By the way, what's wrong with your sister? What's this mood you were talking about?"

Angela laid a finger across her mouth. Taking Serylda's hand, she started them walking again. Serylda looked back and saw why. The rear guards were nearly upon them. A few moments later Angela answered Serylda's question.

"She's jealous of me right now, and I don't know why," she lied. Of course, she knew why. She wasn't ready to confide in Serylda about her feelings for Avery, let alone Alison's feelings.

"Does she do this a lot?" Serylda asked. "I didn't notice that when I taught you two about this world."

"Not really. Don't get me wrong. When I need her, she's there, especially during hard times."

"It must be nice to have someone you can rely upon. Being the king's only daughter has its disadvantages. For example, no one feels comfortable with me. I don't have a close friend … never did." Serylda looked at her feet. "I envy you."

"Yes … well. I can't imagine life without her. Even with all her faults." Angela smiled and tightened her grip on Serylda's hand a second before letting it go. "Now you have a friend. Me. And you can help me right now. I've never felt comfortable asking anyone this. I can see the resemblance between you, Barak, and Devlak. How does Telek fit in? I thought he may be a brother the way he's always near Barak. But with that blond hair I'm not sure. Is he?"

Serylda laughed. "Hardly. He's Barak's personal bodyguard and close friend since childhood. They grew up and learned all they know together. Telek never leaves my brother's side."

Walking in silence for a short time, Angela's thoughts focused on the elf accompanying them. "Do you know anything about Avery?"

"He's another close friend of Barak's. They have fought Ahriman many times, each saving the other more than once." Serylda smiled. "There's more, but I'll leave that for Avery to tell you."

"Okay. Then tell me about the elves in general."

"They're fair-skinned like Avery and have either blond or red hair. You'll be meeting some when we arrive in Krikor." She glanced at Angela. "You'll learn about Ahriman, too."

"Can't you tell me anything about him?"

"I'll try to give you the scaled-down version since we're traveling now. Several thousand years ago, people from the stars came down to Earth to help us. We had nearly destroyed ourselves with pollution. Anyway, Ahriman wanted total control of the planet and the people as his slaves. The off-worlders, as we call them, didn't agree. Ahriman rebelled and caused a great war. The off-worlders disappeared after that. Ahriman has grown stronger since then. And we still fight his armies. That's pretty much it. Avery will tell you more about him. His people kept track of the early days after the war."

Angela suddenly shivered. "Avery scares me a little."

"Why?"

"I don't know. Maybe it's the way he stared at me earlier." She didn't tell Serylda that Avery enchanted her. She wasn't ready to acknowledge her affection for the elf to anyone yet. Besides, she didn't want to think about Alison's jealousy concerning him right now either.

Serylda chuckled. "He does tend to overwhelm at times. Don't worry. If you're truly the Alastrine Savior, and I believe you are, he'll be your personal guard and keep you safe until it's time for you to confront Ahriman."

Whatever that means, Angela thought and hoped it didn't entail killing.

After they had walked all day, Angela's feet hurt. The desert sun had been warm—more like hot, actually. If it hadn't been for the cape she wore, she felt she'd have been roasted by now. She saw a few more trees, but it was still a desert that greeted her eyes that afternoon. She wished they'd stop. *Barak must not believe in taking short rests.*

He called a halt after the sun dipped beneath the horizon. Everyone helped erect tents in a circle, and then they built a fire in the center. Part of the weight of Angela's pack was bedding. She found someone had packed her a few items of underclothes and other essentials along with another set of breeches and a tunic. She promised herself she'd find out who had done it and thank the person. After helping set up the tent she and Alison would use, Angela went to help with the evening meal.

Hadek put a kettle filled with water on the roaring fire. He put her to work peeling and cutting potatoes while he worked on the onions and rabbit meat. After all was cut and ready, he put them into the kettle and seasoned the stew. With everything cooking, he sat on the nearby ground and waited.

Angela made herself comfortable on a log someone had placed near the fire. Alison and Barak joined her on the log. Helmet off and hair brushed back, Barak looked less intimidating. The others strolled over and huddled nearby sitting on the ground. Avery stood a little off to one side, watching the goings-on still wrapped in his cape. The day's heat hadn't seemed to have affected him as it had the rest of the company.

"Barak, I understand Ahriman had a lot of power. What happened to give him so much?" Angela asked. She wasn't ready to ask Avery. She hoped the dwarf could answer.

"We're supposed to wait until we arrive at Krikor to inform you of all we know about Ahriman." Barak studied her a moment and then glanced over at Devlak. "Since we are on our way to Krikor now, you can answer her."

Devlak nodded. "Over two thousand years ago, a spaceship was seen over the Earth. Creatures with pointed ears landed and said they could help us with our problems."

Angela peeked over at Avery. He stared at the ground, the hood of his cape now covering his head.

"What problems?" Alison's voice brought Angela's attention back to the discussion.

"We were destroying the world with pollution. They cautioned us to heal it or face the same consequences they did. They had lost their world and were looking for another to colonize.

"Since we already occupied this world and were destroying it as they had theirs, they had compassion for us. Our world wasn't as far gone as theirs was. They would help us in exchange for the opportunity to use our world as a stopover. They needed rest, and received permission to use some island to the west.

"Then one of their kind disappeared. A month passed. When he reappeared, he had turned evil. He wanted control of the Earth and all its inhabitants. He told the others to cooperate or he'd destroy them. When they didn't agree, he destroyed their ship with a weapon he had made. A second sun appeared in the sky where the ship was supposed to be circling. The few here on Earth were stranded."

"That sounds as if he had an atomic bomb," said Alison.

Telek continued the story. "After the ship was destroyed, Ahriman started the war that destroyed all that was."

"World War Three," Angela said. Alison nodded.

"It became nearly impossible to live on the surface of the Earth in places," Telek said. "We whom you see as dwarves escaped underground along with a few of the off-worlder's worker class, as you know from your studies with Serylda. With the mingling of our bloods, we became the Dwarven Nations of this world. We know not how the humans and elves survived."

"I heard the elves also have off-worlder blood coursing in their veins," Hadek said. "That's why their ears are pointed and they can sometimes know what you think."

"Is that true, Avery?" Alison asked. He shrugged and smiled back at her, not saying a word.

"The Earth had changed, and so did we," Devlak continued. "The great cities were in ruins. Hunger and violence ran rampant. Animals changed too. Some became extinct while others adapted. One animal, the badgercat, is one that escaped their ships. It isn't native to Earth."

"What's a badgercat?" Alison asked.

"Only the most vicious animal around," Barak said. "It's more vicious than a bear. We pointed out the tracks of one to you earlier, remember?"

"Well, if they're that vicious, I hope to never meet one," Angela said. She remembered the huge tracks she'd seen in the sand earlier in the day. They had reminded her of cat tracks, but they were much larger, and the long claws had left huge marks, making the tracks appear even larger.

"Ever since the Great War, we've been in conflict with Ahriman," said Telek. "I hope one of you is indeed the Savior sent to destroy him."

"Excuse me. One more question," Alison began but was interrupted.

Barak rose, ending the conversation. "No more. I think it's time for bed. We have a long way to go yet. Good night, all."

———〜〜ᴑᴏᴄ❁ᴛᴏ❁ᴛᴏ❁ᴏᴑ〜〜———

The next morning Avery began Angela's knife training. From where she practiced, Angela noticed Alison pouting and tried to ignore her, concentrating on Avery's instructions. He made her stab a cactus over and over until she felt sorry for the poor plant. He showed her the proper stances to use that would provide the most advantage in a conflict. She worked at it until she heard Hadek announce, "Breakfast is ready!"

After the meal, everyone pitched in and broke down camp. The trek to Krikor once again got underway. Barak had been right; they had a long way yet to go. This was the first of many campsites they would make on their journey east.

CHAPTER 3

The Storm

T HE SCENERY HAD CHANGED SINCE they'd left Jasper over three
weeks ago. Barak showed Angela a map of the area. According
to him, it was the start of the stormy season, and the area they were
traversing boasted the most severe storms. She thought she recognized
the country. They were somewhere south of the Red River in what
was eastern Texas. The trees closed in on them, becoming thicker the
farther they traveled.

From time to time she glimpsed the wildlife around them. There
were numerous tracks crossing the trail they followed. She recognized
several belonging to badgercats. As time passed, her curiosity got
the better of her. Now, she wanted to see one. But remembering how
vicious Barak said they were, she kept quiet.

The clouds they had seen intermittently between the trees began
to converge. She hated storms. Her thoughts turned to the tornado
that took her family's house when she was a young child. Since
then, she'd cowered from the lightning and thunder that naturally
accompanied storms. She was glad Alison was near. Even though
Alison had experienced the same tornado, storms didn't seem to affect
her. Her devil-may-care attitude always gave Angela courage to face
the occasional stormy weather.

Thinking of Alison seemed to draw her to Angela.

"Getting nervous?" Alison smiled.

Angela nodded. "I'm glad you're here." She took hold of Alison's
arm for comfort.

"I know," Alison said, "you believe it'll turn really bad."

"Well, look at those clouds. You know how I am with
thunderstorms!"

"I'd like to see how these dwarves would react to a tornado," Alison mused.

"Please, I'd rather talk about something else." Angela let her arm drop. "I wonder how much longer we have to go before we reach Krikor. I never realized how far it was to actually walk through several states. And we haven't got through Texas yet."

"Yeah, but remember, there are no states now." Alison leaned closer. "Have you noticed their shoes?" She pointed at Barak's feet. "They remind me of moccasins, not as comfortable as our sneakers. But I'm afraid mine are getting holes in the bottoms."

"Mine too. We need to talk to Barak about that. I bet he'd have something for us," replied Angela. "These tunics sure are more comfortable than I'd first thought."

"I wonder what they do in the winter for footwear," Alison said as she fondled her sword. "I also wonder what kind of metal they use. Look at this sword." She pulled it partway from the scabbard and twisted it this way and that way, making Angela thankful her sister hadn't drawn it all the way out. Alison let it drop to her side. She smiled at Angela and then frowned. "What's wrong now?"

Angela took a deep breath and let it out. "What do you think?"

"It was still tied to my waist and in its scabbard." Alison patted the weapon. "I know how to handle this properly. Devlak taught me well."

"That's not it," Angela stated apprehensively. "I just hope we don't have to fight. I still don't believe I could kill anyone." She thought about the knife tied to her own waist and the bow and arrows strapped to her back. A shudder went through her.

"I could. So don't get in my way." Alison moved closer to Angela. "These dwarves are so trusting," she whispered. "What would keep us from chopping a few of their heads off and disappearing, huh?"

Surprised by her sister's words, Angela stared at her twin and barely missed walking into a clump of nasty-looking briars that seemed to be overtaking the trail. Alison pulled her out of harm's way. Regaining her balance, Angela thanked her sister who just shrugged her shoulders.

Alison rolled her eyes. "I bet I could take on two or three at a time," she said.

"Alison, what is wrong with you?" Angela grabbed her arm. "You're acting strange, even for you! I don't believe that you'd really kill someone. Besides, these people are all we have at the moment. They trust us. You said so yourself. Let's not ruin that, okay?"

Alison laughed. "Don't worry, sis. I'm just joking. Lighten up, will you?"

I sure hope so, Angela thought sullenly. Alison was smart enough to not cause trouble. They had enough to worry about. All this nonsense about one of them being some kind of savior made her nervous enough as it was. Butterflies swarmed in her stomach whenever she thought about it.

What if it's true, though? Will I be forced to kill? Could I? It seems that my sister wants the opportunity. If this Ahriman is so powerful, why can't these dwarves do it? They're strong. I'm not. Besides, what right do they have to expect us to kill someone we really know nothing about?

It was unfair of the dwarves to think that way. She and her sister were just two ordinary girls lost in time. Whereas the dwarves, at home in this time, were warriors.

Startled by thunder, Angela looked up and moaned. The clouds were angry, dark, and restless. She didn't look forward to getting drenched. Hopefully, it probably wouldn't last long.

She thought about talking with Serylda, or rather Darik. So far, no one in the company had guessed another woman was with them, not even Alison. She glanced over at her sister wondering what she was plotting now. Alison was deep in thought, and she knew Alison was becoming jealous of her friendship with Darik.

Angela sighed. Every time she made a new friend, Alison thought she should be part of the group. Couldn't her sister find her own friends? They might be twins, but at times, Angela wished it were different. She knew it would hurt Alison's feelings if she ever discovered how Angela felt. Angela didn't care anymore. Alison would just have to get over it.

The company came to a standstill. The forest surrounding them had become impossible to move through. Nonetheless, Angela caught glimpses of iron girders and half-fallen buildings in the distance. *An ancient Dallas*, she thought. A river appeared to their left running eastward. Avery had called it the Red River. Yes, they were definitely in Tornado Alley. Still, she was grateful for the halt.

"You've got to be kidding," Alison was saying. "We are camping here? We'll get soaked. Can't you find a better place?"

Barak stared at Alison a minute and then turned away to help set up camp. As he did so, it began to drizzle. The dwarves, handy with their axes, cleared an area large enough for their camp. Everything was wet before the company finished their preparations for the night. This campsite was going to be their first miserable one since their journey began. Angela didn't complain. They'd been lucky so far.

Angela studied the campsite from her tent door. Hadek worked on the fire for the evening meal. She heard Telek volunteer to do the cooking, and he went in search of meat. *He does wonderful things with meat*, she mused. She never saw Hadek harbor jealousy toward Telek taking over when he did.

It had quit raining when Telek returned. He carried several large rabbits and some herbs he'd found. Angela's mouth watered as she left her shelter. She'd eat her fair share tonight.

Although the rain had let up, the water fell in big drops from branches and leaves overhead. The insects renewed their incessant chatter. The thunder occasionally joined in. The river flowed lazily by, its bed so wide it had plenty of room to spread out. She desperately wanted a bath. But the river was just as silt ridden now as it had been in her time—a testament to the fact that it still was called by the original name.

Barak and Devlak moved some logs next to the fire. Angela sat down on the driest one, and Barak settled next to her. Surprisingly, Angela found her cape had kept her dry. Devlak moved off to talk to some of the other dwarves.

"How much farther do we have to go?" Angela asked Barak.

"If we're as lucky as we've been and don't meet with any of Ahriman's men, we should be in Krikor in a few more weeks."

"We have been pretty lucky," Telek said. "I'm surprised how far we've come. This is the fastest trip I can recall in a long time." He finished putting the meat on a spit, and with Hadek's help, hung it over the fire.

"Good weather aided us there, I think," Devlak chimed in.

"Well, I'll be glad when we get there," Alison added. She sat down next to Angela. "I'm getting sick of all this camping."

"You?" Angela's eyebrows knitted together. "I'm the one that usually complained about camping. You always enjoyed it."

"Yeah, but only for a few days, not weeks. And our shoes are worn out." She showed Barak her shoe bottoms.

"You will have to get by for now," he said. "But, I'll have Sasek improvise some soles for you tomorrow."

Alison snorted.

Angela's stomach growled. A few eyes turned in her direction. The aroma of freshly cooking meat smelled so good.

"Hungry?" asked Telek, a smile on his face.

She nodded and returned his smile. He was friendly, and she enjoyed his company. He pulled another log near and sat down.

She shivered suddenly. She felt eyes upon her, and not from any of the dwarves. Could someone be watching them from the darkness of the forest? She looked over at Alison who looked to be obsessed over her shoes. Other than that, nothing bothered her. Suddenly the forest didn't feel right to Angela.

"Barak," she inquired, "does this forest have a name?"

"Yes. We call it the Adricon Forest. It means 'dark forest.' Ahriman had control of it for centuries. That is, until we rooted him out."

"That name suits it." Thunder boomed in the distance. Angela shivered. It promised to be a long and stormy night. "What happened?" she asked in an attempt to keep her mind off the impending storm.

"Ahriman destroyed most of the life here. He experimented with the animals. I heard he did something genetically to the badgercat—a gentle pet to the Ancient Ones—and made it vicious. So, twenty or so years ago, Avery and I led an army to drive him out. It was our first campaign together." He studied the surroundings and sighed. "I'm surprised he hasn't come back. No one has been here in years."

"Why didn't you tell us that earlier about the badgercat?" Alison asked.

Angela laid a hand on her sister's arm. She was becoming snappish with Barak, and Angela didn't want an argument along with the impending storm.

"It wasn't important," he said.

Lightning flashed. The storm drew nearer. Angela heard an owl hoot in the distance, competing with the noise of the insects and the storm. She was getting more nervous, but surprisingly, she wasn't worried. As long as the insects kept up their chatter, she felt safe.

Devlak joined their gathering. The rest of the company milled about, finding other logs to use as seats. He leaned over the fire to get a whiff of the cooking meat and then turned the spit for Telek.

Barak rose and joined his brother. "I still think Father shouldn't have let you come along." His eyebrows knitted together. He took a stick, squatted down, and began poking the fire, sending sparks skyward. The fire sizzled whenever the rabbit juices dripped onto it unobstructed by Barak's ministrations.

"And miss out on all the fun, brother?" Devlak grinned. "No way. Besides, Father believed I was in need of a little battle training. Remember?" Devlak winked at Angela and sat down on a nearby log. "And although we haven't seen any of Ahriman's men, you may still need my help."

Angela looked down, trying to keep a straight face. Brothers were the same no matter where—or when—a girl found herself. It was a comforting thought. Barak kept poking the fire while the rest of the company waited for the coneys to finish cooking.

After supper everyone pitched in for the cleanup, as had been the custom for the entire trip. Soon all the bones were buried and the individual plates were wiped clean and stowed. The storm hadn't let loose its deluge yet, though thunder still rumbled ominously. So, after stowing the spit into his pack, Hadek brought out an elaborately carved flute. Sitting on the log next to Angela, he began playing. Barak, on another log nearby, puffed on his pipe, his eyes closed in contemplation. Some of the men played some sort of game behind her. Alison relaxed next to her watching Avery. Avery, Telek, and Devlak looked to be having an interesting conversation. At times their laughter rang out louder than the thunder.

Angela enjoyed listening to Hadek play. She wished he'd play more often. His music soothed her nerves, allowing her mind to wander back to her former life. She missed the friends she had. *And, you miss the ease of living then too,* she reminded herself. *No turning on a faucet for water or electricity for refrigeration here.* True, the time Alison and she spent studying in Jasper had helped her adjust, but she couldn't forget what she had lost. Her friends were dead a long time now. *I wonder how long they searched for us before giving up.*

Hadek stopped playing for a moment, interrupting her musings.

"Where did you learn to play like that?" she asked.

"Avery taught me when I was a small child. It kept me busy and out of the trouble I usually found myself getting into." He returned to his flute and played another tune.

Angela closed her eyes and let her imagination run. The tents, arranged in a circle, the chain mail and weapons, the storm … they all combined to produce an eerie feeling in her. Suddenly, goose bumps slid up and down her arms. She must be losing her mind. She shook her head to try to clear out the fanciful scenes.

"I've decided to give you your knife lesson now while the rain has slackened." Breaking into her musings, Avery stood in front of her.

At that Alison stomped off to the edge of camp. Angela sighed. Alison was becoming obsessive over herself and Avery. Not wanting to bring Avery's attention to her sister, she nodded and rose.

After they had worked for a while, Avery complimented her. "You've learned a lot since Jasper. You're nearly ready for combat."

"Am I that good?" She found talking to Avery was easy … when he instructed. He acted very professionally, which put her at ease and made it effortless for her to ignore her own feelings concerning both combat and the elf.

"Tonight I will teach you how to disarm your opponent."

He took her knife and laid it on the log next to Barak. Then, he picked up two sticks and handed her the shorter of the two. She took up her position as he had taught her, with the stick as her weapon. He checked her stance as he talked.

"I'm giving you the shorter stick for a reason. When you've mastered the art of disarming your opponent with it, you will be more effective with a longer one. Now, do you remember how I taught you to hold your knife?" As she demonstrated what she remembered, he continued his teaching. "In a firm, but relaxed grip. Good. Your enemy will be more experienced than you, so be sure you have your bow or a long stick nearby. You can use them to aid in disarming your enemy. Like this …"

He took the other stick and showed her how to come down onto her opponent's wrist. He instructed her to carry through with what he just showed her.

"What if I hurt you?"

"Don't worry. I am teaching you the way I was taught. Now, disarm me."

She made a feeble attempt, still worried about injuring him.

"Angela, put your heart into it. Right now, I'm your enemy. Knock this 'knife' from my hand."

He wove to and fro and made it hard for her to achieve her goal. He kept her hopping. She was getting frustrated when at last she saw her chance. Swinging her stick in a wide arch, she brought it down across his wrist. Her stick broke while his went flying.

She grinned before she noticed him wince. *Oh, no. Did I break his wrist?* She dropped what was left of her stick to check Avery's injury. Probing, she checked for fractures. "I was afraid of this. I hope it's not broken."

He smiled. "You need not worry. It's not broken. I forgot I was training an adult, not a child. The pain has nearly subsided."

His hand felt good beneath her fingers, warm to the touch. She lost sense of where she was until thunder boomed and startled her. *Goodness, I'm still holding his hand!* She let it go in a hurry. Lightning lit up the camp and Angela saw Alison stomp off into the storm. Hadek quit playing as it began sprinkling.

Avery nodded toward the direction Alison had gone. "She is angry," he said, "at us both."

Angela sighed. "I know. She's my sister. I'd better see what her problem is."

"I understand. We'll cut our lesson short this evening. You're learning well and fast. Go and talk to your sister. But don't wander too far from camp. I sense trouble nearby." He turned and joined the others near the fire.

Angela shook her head and started off in the direction Alison had taken. She didn't know what to do with that girl at times. And the storm was so near. Why did she have to walk so far from camp? She called but received no answer. Well, she'd just have to brave the storm and find Alison.

Where is that dratted girl? Barak had told them not to wander too far from camp. And Avery had cautioned her, because he sensed trouble. Did he sense the storm, a badgercat, or something worse? Granted, they hadn't seen any signs of enemy troops since first beginning their journey. That didn't mean there wasn't any danger. She had spotted badgercat tracks just outside the campsite. Angela hadn't been able to get the thought of a badgercat out of her mind since spotting those particular tracks.

A flash of lightning followed by a crack of thunder pursued her deeper into the forest. Silently she wished Avery was beside her, but really didn't want to think of him. Alison was acting irrationally because of him. She knew it wasn't her fault her sister had turned mean, and she didn't want him in the middle of that.

"Alison, come on. Where are you?" Angela whispered as she pulled her hood over her hair. *Drat that girl!* "Alison!" she called loudly.

Angela jumped, startled at a distinct plop in the river. The sound originated from her right, from the north. She spotted Alison sitting on a rock that hung over the river several hundred paces from camp. The trees provided ample cover from the rain and hid the location well. At least Alison had chosen a good spot, with more protection than they had at the campsite.

Angela walked to the base of the rock and looked up about ten feet to where Alison sat. "What are you doing out here? You know we aren't supposed to wander so far from camp. Remember how dangerous it can be? Remember the badgercat tracks? Avery told me before I came looking for you that he sensed trouble nearby."

"Why can't you stay away from him?" Alison sullenly threw another rock into the river. She looked angrily at Angela, the storm mirrored in her eyes. "Avery will be mine. He'll never be yours."

"Alison, you know as well as I that he's his own person. Anyway, he's to protect whichever one of us is this so-called savior. In a way I hope it's you, but we don't know yet. We won't know until we reach Krikor. Why be jealous now? Calm down and wait until our future is a little clearer."

"You say that even though you're trying your hardest to be that person," Alison grumbled. "I saw how you held his hand, and the look you gave him made me sick!" She made an immature gagging motion. Then she turned back to the river, picked up another rock, and threw it into the dark water. She shouted belligerently over her shoulder as lightning lit up the area, "I want him and he will be mine! So stay out of my way, dear sister, or you might get hurt!"

Angela jumped at nature's sound. The wind picked up and blew in violent gusts, tugging at her cape, and thunder gave emphasis to the storm. The trees no longer provided cover from the rain that beat down in great cold sheets.

"All right, Alison." Angela looked at the sky and tried to shout above the noise of the storm. "We need to get back. This storm is getting worse. It's dangerous."

"Afraid, sis?" Alison taunted and laughed.

"Well, yes." Angela spread her hands apart imploringly. "C'mon, Alison. This storm is too hazardous. We shouldn't be out in it like this."

Self-pityingly, Alison looked out over the water. "I couldn't care less."

"Do you really not care if you get hurt out here—or worse, killed?"

"Why should I care? We don't have a home anymore."

Struggling through the wind and rain, Angela climbed up until she made it to her twin's side. She sat down next to her. At times, Alison became so self-centered it grated on Angela's nerves. "Okay, talk to me. What's really wrong? There's more to it than your obsession with Avery."

Dejected, Alison began, "Well, that is part of it." She picked up yet another rock but fingered it instead of throwing it. "I talked to Avery last night when he was on watch. I couldn't help it." She disgustedly threw the rock. The rumble of thunder drowned out the plop of the rock. "I came on to him again, and he blew me off. Said I was still too forward. And—" Thunder drowned out her next words. "And he told me something I was to keep to myself. But, you know what? I don't care. I'll tell you anyway. He said you—"

A nearby tree exploded as it was struck by lightning. Both girls were instantly knocked to the ground. At the same instant, the bushes came alive. Men dressed in black emerged from the forest.

Angela grabbed for her knife, remembering too late it was sitting beside Barak back at camp. After a short scuffle, the girls found their hands tied behind their backs, and each was summarily slung over the shoulders of a smelly man. Angela kicked at her captor to no avail. He wrapped his arms tightly around her legs, hampering her movements. The man laughed at her feeble attempts to escape while the stink emanating from him made her gag. *At least the dwarves have the sense to bathe when it's possible,* she thought.

In the distance, the sound becoming fainter as they retreated, she discerned her comrades engaged in a heated battle. Regrettably, here she was, easily captured, unable to do anything, because she was too far from camp.

The man carrying Angela moved into the river. Suddenly, she found herself submerged, unable to breathe. She struggled violently until her captor brought her head out of the water. Able to breathe again, she ceased her struggle. *At least he doesn't intend for me to drown!*

After they reached the other side, she was set on her feet. Ten horses tethered to nearby trees waited for them. She struggled as her captor pulled a rope from the saddlebags and retied her hands in front of her. He positioned the knot on the outside of her wrists where it made it impossible for her to untie it with her teeth.

Tears streamed down her cheeks and mingled with the rain. Nine other men joined them. One dragged Alison and bound her the same way Angela was bound. Both were lifted into saddles, and their captors mounted up behind them.

With the two horses carrying double, the group headed north. In the dark of night as lightning flashed and thunder boomed, they traveled away from the river to some unknown destination … while Angela's tears were washed away by the storm.

CHAPTER 4

Captives

AFTER A FEW MILES OF hard riding in a northerly direction, the men turned their horses east. Decrepit buildings came into view now and then as they came upon an ancient roadway. The huge slabs of concrete sat in twin rows. *This is I-35,* Angela thought. *We're in Oklahoma.* She had hoped to be rescued by now. Having lived in Ardmore, Oklahoma, when she was in middle school, she knew the area well. According to the map she remembered seeing in Jasper, Krikor was nearly due east from their present location.

They turned north again, using the ancient roadway. They hadn't gone far when the horse Alison and her captor shared collapsed. The rest of the army rode on.

"What's the matter?" Angela's captor grunted.

"Damned horse fell into a hole. Broke his leg." The man struggled to his feet and kicked the poor beast.

"Well!" Angela's captor laughed. "Looks like you and her gets to walk." He grabbed Angela and pushed her off. She fell with her hands still tied, her knee catching her fall. She picked herself up and moaned. Her knee hurt; she hoped it wasn't badly damaged.

"Go on. Get over there." He prodded her from astride his horse with his booted foot. A few tears escaped and ran down her cheeks. She steeled herself. She didn't want to give him the satisfaction of seeing her weak, or crying out from the pain in her knee.

The clouds began to break up. Enough moonlight shone through and Angela caught a glimpse of their captors. They were filthy. No wonder they stank.

"Tie their hands together," Angela's captor ordered.

"We got to make sure they don't die."

"We also got to get farther from them nasty dwarves. The moon's showing us up." The two men glared at each other. "Brud, it was your horse that got hurt. Do what I said."

"Oh, yes, mighty Galth," Brud said derisively with a scowl. He bowed and did as he had been told. Retrieving another rope from the suffering horse, he tied a loop in the center. He tied one end around each girl's waist and handed the looped center to Galth; then he climbed behind Galth on the remaining horse.

Galth urged the beast forward, pulling the girls along. Angela looked back at the abandoned horse. It cried piteously from its pain. The least they could have done was put it out of its misery. Angela's fear and hatred for these men turned to rage. She consoled herself with the fact she didn't have to ride with that stinky Galth. She would escape somehow. Then she would seek revenge on Galth for herself, Alison, and that poor horse back there. *He seems to be the ringleader*, she noted silently. *It's his fault.*

Tripping over a weed, Angela barely missed falling again. Alison helped her regain her footing. Galth looked back and smirked. He didn't slow down.

Angela could blame their predicament on Alison easily. If she had stayed in camp, they wouldn't be in this mess. But that wasn't fair to her twin. From the sounds of battle she'd heard earlier, she felt they might have been taken hostage at camp anyway. And she had to take some of the blame. She had left herself defenseless.

Her thoughts turned to Serylda and the others. Was she okay? Did anyone survive? She prayed Avery was alive and hunting for them.

As the eastern sky lightened, they halted. The men ahead had set up camp. The girls were led to a tree and tied to it. Although their hands were no longer tied, the knots in the rope around their waists were inaccessible to either girl. They were each given a beaker of brackish water and a plate that held a stale piece of bread and some meat. Neither girl touched the rotten meat. After their meager meal, they fell into a deep, uncomfortable sleep, more exhausted than either would admit. Someone kicked them awake later in the afternoon and gave them their ration of bread and water—but no meat this time.

The afternoon sky clouded over with another threat of thunderstorms. It promised to be another miserable night for the twins. For some reason Angela had no apprehension about the weather. Her fear seemed to be gone. Their predicament was more frightening than even the threat of tornadoes.

Angela moaned. She was sore everywhere, especially her knee. It was pretty badly bruised. Her body ached from sleeping against the tree. The exhaustion from the night before was still with her also, and it didn't help when Galth and Brud yanked them to their feet.

"Easy, man!" Alison kicked Brud hard on his shin, emphasizing her words. He returned the favor by slapping her face so hard it knocked her to the ground.

Galth laughed, doubled over from his mirth.

"Shut up!" Brud said as he pulled Alison to her feet none too gently. "I said stop your laughing."

"Time to go," Galth said with one more guffaw.

The men tied the girls with separate ropes this time. Galth took control of Angela while Brud pulled Alison along. The rest of the men were well ahead of them by now and nearly lost from sight. All of them on foot this time, the men hurried them along. Now and then they passed decrepit buildings that stood near the roadway as they made their way north. Unknown to the girls, the ancient town of Ardmore lay a half day's march away.

Wait. What happened to the horses? Angela looked around and remembered. Earlier in the day she'd heard a commotion. Too tired to do anything except open one eye, she'd seen the men chasing the horses. The animals had escaped. She smiled for the horses. Too bad they hadn't been as lucky. She felt a small sense of justice knowing their captors had to walk with them.

In other circumstances she would have noticed her surroundings. A beautiful spring morning greeted them despite the threat of more storms. The birds sang, and a cool breeze blew the heavy clouds around like playthings. But her thoughts stayed on their predicament. Her wrists hurt. Galth had tied the rope too tight. It cut off her circulation; her fingers felt numb.

"I'm thirsty." Alison's raspy words cut into her thoughts.

"Shut up!" yelled Brud.

"No. I'm thirsty!" She mimicked Brud's rough voice. Alison repeated her request until Brud tugged her rope hard enough to knock her off her feet. He dragged her several yards before allowing her to regain her footing.

Angela was thirsty, too, but dared not say anything. Galth looked mad enough to tackle a grizzly. He'd probably do worse than drag her along like Brud had done to Alison.

Tears ran freely down her face. She didn't care who saw them. Where were Avery and the others? Were they even hunting for them? Or were they all dead? No! She couldn't think like that. They were alive ... had to be. She'd blame herself if they weren't.

Thunder boomed in the distance. Strange, it didn't seem to frighten her. She didn't care. She hung her head. *We are doomed, right? So why worry about a measly storm?*

She stopped crying, startled by her thoughts. She was alive. She could not give up. She remembered her promise to herself. There may come a time when she could escape. She had to be ready for it. She focused her mind on that possibility.

Galth pulled her close. "Maybe, you and me can have some fun later, eh?" His loathsome grin showed missing and rotten teeth, and his breath was worse than the odor emanating from his body, if that were possible.

Fun? Angela's eyes grew big. Her heart beat in double time to her steps. No. She wouldn't allow him to violate her body.

Brud chuckled. "Great idea, man. But, we better be careful. The others will tattle to the Big Man."

"Yeah," Galth agreed. "But, who'd know if we take them into a building and then have our fun, eh? We're stopping at that abandoned town up ahead."

Brud yanked Alison's rope, bringing her close. "I haven't had a good romp in a long time," he leered. "I hope you fight good." Alison struggled. She managed a decent hard kick aimed at Galth's shin, but she missed her target. Brud laughed.

"Shut up!" Galth yelled. His voice carried to the men up ahead. They glanced back, returning to their march only when Galth glared at them.

Brud laughed louder. "I bet you hope yours is as feisty as mine."

Galth didn't bother to answer.

The wind blew in gusts as the storm neared. Angela, her mind on Galth's earlier threat, barely registered the decrepit buildings that closed in on them. An hour more of marching brought them to the outskirts of the ancient town.

It also brought the rain in torrents. Small hailstones fell with the rain and pelted everyone painfully. More than once Angela heard one of Galth's men cry out. One hailstone hit Angela on her left shoulder and numbed her whole arm. She didn't cry out, and felt superior to the men.

Everyone began running when the hail grew in size and intensity. The girls kept tripping and were dragged by their captors. After several falls, the men picked the girls up, threw them over their shoulders, and ran. With the stink of Galth's body and the jostling she received, Angela heaved. Thankfully her stomach was empty. But, if he didn't stop, she would die.

Galth chose a building away from the others. He placed Angela on the floor and peered out. Assured no one would interfere, he snickered and came close. "Now we can have our fun. Heh, heh."

Angela screamed. Her courage flew out the building. Galth laughed and grabbed her by her collar.

"Scream all you like. Nobody will hear. The storm's too loud. Anyway, I like my women to fight. Show me what you're made of."

He pulled her close. His foul breath in her nostrils made her gag. She tried moving her head away. He took hold of it and forced her to look at him. When he leaned forward to kiss her, she surprised herself. She bit his lower lip so hard she drew blood. He bellowed and slapped her to the ground. She hit hard, saw stars, and spat blood.

"I'll show you, you little witch!" He landed on top of her and knocked what breath she had out of her body. He grabbed a handful of hair and yanked hard. "Don't do that again."

She glared. *What's happened to my fear?* He was going to rape her. Having never known a man in that sense should have left her rigid with fear. But the rage she felt earlier built to bursting. She wasn't going down without a fight.

Only one problem stopped her. He was on top of her and he was heavy—near two hundred pounds. Her small physique was useless. The panic returned. She moaned as Galth tore at her tunic. The wind howled with fury outside.

Wait, she thought. The wind was deafening. She knew that sound. A tornado! Their time was up. Was she about to die with this stinking excuse for a man on top of her? She didn't want to die like that. She pushed Galth with strength she never knew she possessed. She raised him an inch off herself. Then it struck.

Angela screamed. Her voice joined the scream of the tornado as it tore their shelter apart. The building shook. They looked up in time to see the roof disappear. The building buckled around them, trapping them, crushing them. Suddenly, silence enveloped them. Galth tried to move and then lay still.

She tried pushing him off to no avail. She was trapped. Something sticky and warm trickled across her shoulders. Blood? Hers or Galth's? He moved, still alive.

Something creaked before the remainder of the building collapsed. Galth took one last breath and struggled no more.

Angela panted, her breath ragged. She was alive by some miracle. But how? She pushed at Galth's body once more. He was pinned on top of her. She felt panic rise within her. Trying to move her foot, she cried out in sudden pain. Something had her caught.

She quit her struggling and thought of the irony that a tornado had somehow saved her. She had survived, albeit in extreme pain. And that was her last thought before she slipped into blissful unconsciousness.

CHAPTER 5

The Rescue

ANGELA FELT WARM SUNSHINE ON her legs. She ached everywhere. How long had she been out? She tried to shift her position and cried out in pain. Galth's body crushing hers didn't help. Something stabbed into her right arm. Tears streamed down her face. She stopped her struggling.

She felt cold despite the sun's warmth. The only thing she could do was sleep, but try as she might, she had no luck. She hurt too much.

Time dragged on. She slept restlessly through the night. By morning she began to doubt being rescued. She forced herself not to give up. *I am alive, right? I have to believe and hope for a rescue. Someone will show. Avery will rescue me.*

A tear escaped and slid down her cheek. It opened a floodgate. *Now why am I crying? Why can't I stop?* Yes, she was trapped. *But I am alive!* She kept repeating that to herself.

Her thoughts turned to Alison. Had her twin escaped death? What had happened to her? She could really use Alison's strength right now. She cried herself to sleep worrying about her twin's circumstance.

She awoke from the unexpected but much-needed nap. She felt better for it. Something had awakened her, though. Galth? He stank worse than before. That wasn't it.

Then she heard her name. It was very faint. Was it friend or foe? Or was she dreaming it? She'd been here quite some time now. How much blood had she lost? *Does that cause a person to start hallucinating?*

She heard her name again, only louder. It was Avery! She recognized his voice. Her own voice croaked when she tried to cry out. Her throat was too dry. She searched round with her left hand until she felt a loose piece of metal. She wrapped her hand around it and used it like a hammer, pounding on a metal girder within her reach. She began to cry. It was useless, barely louder than her voice. She didn't have the strength to pound harder.

"Angel, I hear you," Avery said. He was nearby. His voice sounded so heavenly to her ears it sent a fresh wave of tears streaming down her cheeks. She wished he'd hurry. The smell emanating from Galth's body was sickeningly sweet, almost too much for her to bear.

Avery moved into her line of sight. "Don't worry. You'll be free soon."

He grabbed a piece of metal and used it as a lever. Groaning with effort, he moved a huge chunk of debris. Angela felt a weight lift from her chest. She was still pinned—why? Avery threw the metal aside and worked on smaller pieces of debris. Soon, he uncovered Galth's body.

"There seems to be a long piece of metal stabbed into this man and into you. It's what's holding you pinned. Probably what killed the man." He braced himself. "It may hurt when I remove this, Angel. Ready?"

She nodded.

He pulled. She cried out. Her right arm was on fire with pain. How bad her arm was injured she was afraid to know. She closed her eyes and gritted her teeth. Avery finished his grisly job and tossed Galth's body aside. He picked her up and carried her out of the wreckage. The afternoon sun felt so good.

"Don't move, Angel," he said, putting her down gently. "I'll be back."

Taking advantage of Avery's disappearance, she checked her injuries. Her arm had suffered a bad gash and was now bleeding freely. She applied pressure to the wound and finished looking herself over. Nothing seemed broken. The only other wound she'd suffered from the building collapse was a sore ankle. She'd get Avery to look at that.

Shouldn't he be back by now? Where has he gone? And what about Alison? She told herself Alison was fine. She was a fighter. Besides, she couldn't bear to think her sister was dead or dying somewhere nearby.

She heard a rustle adjacent to the next building. Perhaps that was Avery returning. A strange-looking creature peered out. That was not Avery.

"What kind of animal are you?" she whispered, not wanting to frighten it.

The animal stood on all fours, about four feet tall at least. It was covered in a coarse fur that made it look like a giant hedgehog. Its color was a mottled orange and red with a spattering of black thrown in. It sported a dog's muzzle but the slit-pupil eyes of a cat. The eyes were an iridescent orange that made them stand out vividly.

Avery appeared from behind a building across the street. He stopped in his tracks. "Don't make any sudden moves, Angel." His voice barely made it to her ears. "That's a badgercat."

Angela's heart raced at his words. *So, that's a badgercat.* She wouldn't have guessed they were so pretty. She calmed herself down. It hadn't made any threatening moves as far as she could tell. It sniffed the air a few times before scampering off the way it had come.

Cautiously, Avery joined her, his blue eyes darting here and there. "We can't be too careful when it comes to badgercats." He set down a bowl made from half a gourd; it was filled with water. From a pocket he pulled out a piece of cloth and wetted it.

"It didn't seem dangerous to me," she said.

"They have been known to attack without provocation, Angel." He wiped some of the grime from her face. "They are vicious. Please don't be fooled by this particular cat."

She lay quiet as he finished his ministrations. He checked her foot. It had suffered only a bruise; there were no broken bones. The same went for her knee. He checked her arm. He gingerly wiped it clean though it still bled. A piece of metal was still imbedded in the wound. Gently, he pulled it out. He used a piece of his tunic as a bandage and bound the injury.

"The pressure you applied to your arm helped stop most of the bleeding. And the shard that had implanted itself in the wound kept you from bleeding to death. You've been very lucky, all in all. You should recover quickly."

"Thanks." She sat up with his help. "Did you find my sister?"

"No, Angel. Your building was the only one destroyed by the storm. Some trees were uprooted, but the other buildings suffered no damage. No one was in them." He touched her uninjured arm. "I'm sorry, Angel. Your sister is gone, and you are more important than she."

"She's important to me, Avery." Tears streamed down her face once more. Her thoughts turned north; she believed Alison yet lived and felt she was in that direction. Why she felt that she wasn't sure.

"I know. But, you have to be strong." He shook her gently to get her attention. "You are the one with a destiny to fulfill, Angel."

"A destiny?" Angela stopped crying and frowned at him.

He rose and helped her to her feet. "C'mon, let's get you cleaned up a little."

When she applied her weight to her injured foot, she cried out and nearly fainted. Avery picked her up and carried her to a pond a few yards away. He placed her on the ground and went back for his bowl.

When he left, she became aware of her disheveled state. Galth had torn her tunic beyond repair from the rough treatment she had endured. It did little to cover her up. When Avery returned, he handed her his spare tunic as he placed the bowl on the ground.

She thanked him, and as she covered herself up, she asked, "What did you mean by what you said earlier, and why do you keep calling me Angel?"

He changed the water in the bowl and handed it to her.

"Avery?"

"Later," he said. "I'll explain that later." He rose and disappeared again.

Angela used the fresh water to clean herself of the grime she'd accumulated from the storm. She scrubbed at the dirt as best she could with one hand. After ten minutes of toiling she decided that had to do. She felt better and sat back to wait for Avery's return.

Panic began to rise in her. *Avery should be back by now*, she thought. She fell asleep for a while, and when she woke, the sun, high in the sky when Avery left, now hugged the horizon. She willed herself to calm down. Avery had freed her of that stinking Galth. *I can make it to Krikor if I have to, right?* She knew basically where it was. No, she was kidding herself. If Avery didn't return she was doomed to die here.

"I thought you might be hungry." Avery returned and held up a rabbit.

She sighed and nodded. She was famished. He made a fire and put the meat on to cook. Leaving once more, he promised to return before the meat was ready. Angela resigned herself to the wait, a little less apprehensive, and turned the spit so the rabbit would cook evenly. With nothing else to occupy her mind, her thoughts turned once again to her sister. Alison must have survived. Avery had assured her he had found only one body. That was Galth. The other men must have taken her sister north with them.

Then suddenly her thoughts turned to Avery. *Why did he leave this time?* She wondered if he felt her discomfort when he was near. *Did that cause him to disappear for a time?* She recalled Serylda's words concerning the elf's ability to read thoughts. *Was he reading mine when he was near me? How can I shield my thoughts from him if that's true?*

Avery returned, having been gone not as long as before. They feasted on the tasty meat. Angela enjoyed hers so much she forgot her injuries for the time they ate. After cleaning up, Avery picked her up. She protested so much he put her on her feet. He helped her hobble to a nearby building.

"It's nearly too dark to see," he said. "We should be safe in here. I checked the place out. It's wise not to be out in the open—especially with that badgercat roaming around."

She leaned against the doorframe, refusing to move. Avery sat down against a wall and beckoned her over. He patted the ground next to himself.

"Come. I'll be your pillow. You need sleep."

"There?" she squeaked. A familiar panic rose in her.

"Well, yes," he frowned. "I don't understand why you're suddenly afraid of me, Angel. I won't hurt you. You have nothing to fear."

Biding time, she asked, "Why do you keep calling me Angel? You promised me you'd tell me."

He smiled. "Come sit. I'll explain then." He patted the ground again.

Taking a deep breath she did so. He pulled her close and enveloped her in his arms, being careful of her injury.

Angela's heart pounded. Could he feel it? Leaning against him, she realized she had fallen in love with him the moment she'd laid eyes on him. The trek to Krikor only made it grow strong. Realizing how close she was to him, she shifted and squirmed, afraid he was reading her thoughts.

"Easy, Angel." He shifted to ease her discomfort. "I promised you an explanation. First, I want you to know I believe your sister will be fine. She's a fighter. She'll survive." Angela had a hard time believing that but kept quiet, somehow feeling reassured.

"Now. Why do I call you Angel? Because in my heart I believe you are the true Alastrine Savior."

"But, why me? Why was I chosen? Why wasn't my sister the one chosen?"

"I don't have the answer to that. Only Queen Kalika can tell you. She's the keeper of the legend and its history. She'll tell you what you'll need to know."

"I don't like being kept in the dark, but I guess I'll trust you. Thank you, Avery, for everything."

He smiled and leaned back, pulling her with him. "Now, let's sleep. We have a long day in front of us. We start for Krikor before sunup."

Angela awoke to a scratching sound. It was still quite dark, but in the light of the moon she could see the badgercat standing inside the doorway. Was it the same one she'd seen before? It had the same black patch around its right eye. She smiled and shifted slightly to get a better view.

"Shh, don't move, Angel," Avery whispered in her ear.

"What does it want?" she whispered back.

"Who knows? This one is acting strangely."

"At least it doesn't seem to be making any threatening moves."

As before, it rose on its haunches and sniffed the air. In no hurry, it turned and moved out of sight.

Angela sighed. "It's such a beautiful creature. I have a hard time believing it's as vicious as everyone says."

"Don't let the actions of this one fool you, Angel. They are vicious. And when provoked, can claw a grown man to death in minutes. Promise you won't go near one." He made her face him.

"I promise," she said. *Until I find out more about them*, she promised herself.

She lay back down, but after five minutes of fidgeting, she apologized. She couldn't get comfortable. "And I'm wide awake, now," she said. "Any ideas as to how to get back to sleep?"

"I feel the same," he concurred. "We may as well head out now. It'll be light in an hour."

Outside the building, Avery checked Angela's wounds. She looked back and saw the badgercat. It peeked from behind the structure they had just left. She experienced a sensation of having been protected, knowing the cat had been there. Strange. She decided Avery didn't need to know what she'd just felt. Covertly she waved at the creature. They headed out. Angela struggled to walk despite Avery's support.

"This will not do." Avery brought them to a halt after only a few yards. He located a sturdy piece of wood and tied it to her ankle with a piece of the rope Galth had used on her. He fashioned another longer piece of wood into a crutch. She tried to walk with Avery's help and found it more tolerable and a bit easier.

She thanked him. Once more on their way, Avery offered his arm for some support. She accepted, thankful she didn't need to be carried.

"How far is it to Krikor?"

"We should be there in ten to twelve days at this speed. Why?"

"Then it'll be too late to go after Alison, won't it?"

"I'm afraid so, Angel. I'm truly sorry."

A tear slid down her cheek. She didn't see the rock in her path and stepped hard onto it with her bad ankle. She fell, nearly bringing Avery down upon her.

"No!" she cried. "How can I be so clumsy?"

Avery checked her ankle. "It's definitely worse now, badly sprained, if not broken. I can't tell here."

"I'm so sorry. I can't walk. I'm useless. How can I do anything for this world when I can't even get myself to Krikor in one piece?"

"Angel, quit berating yourself." He took her in his arms and held her until she calmed down. "Are you all right now?"

She sniffed once and nodded. "Sorry. I'm usually calm. I don't break down easily. I don't know what the matter is with me."

He wiped a tear from her cheek. She turned to stone, and her eyes widened in surprise. His breath suddenly turned shaky. *Are his feelings like mine?*

"I'd better go make a sled so we can get moving."

He made sure she was comfortable under a protective tree and left. Shortly he returned, dragging two small trees he'd cut down. He stripped off the bark with his knife. He took off his cape and tied it between the poles. After helping Angela onto the sled, he resumed their trek, pulling the sled behind him.

"Avery, what became of my knife? I remember leaving it next to Barak."

"It's with me."

"I feel so guilty."

"You're hurt. Just relax. Try to sleep. Time will pass more swiftly for you."

Avery barely spoke for the remainder of the day and the next. He made frequent stops to rest his arms and allow Angela to sit upright and relieve her boredom. It proved tiresome for them both, and Angela feared her arm was worsening. It throbbed with pain continuously now. She told him when they stopped for the afternoon of the second day. "Something's wrong with my arm. I think it's worse."

After checking her injury, he peered into her face, worried. "I fear for your arm, Angel. If we don't get to Krikor soon, I'm afraid you're going to lose it." He leaned back. "It's my fault you're hurt. I should have gone with you to look for Alison. I felt something was wrong, remember? Yet, I allowed you to go alone." He bowed his head. "I am sorry."

She placed her left hand on his shoulder. "It's not your fault. I believe Ahriman's men would've taken my sister and me hostage at camp. And, you might be dead now. So, don't blame yourself."

He looked into her eyes. "I'll promise you something in return for your promise. I'll stop blaming myself if you do the same."

She chuckled. "Agreed." She sensed her own guilt and recognized his manipulation of her emotions.

He stared into her eyes, mesmerized for a second, then rose. "We'd better get going." He helped her back on the sled, and they resumed their long trek to Krikor.

———

That evening found Angela in delirium. Avery feared she was near death. Her body burned with a high fever. He gathered herbs and brewed a tea. Rousing her, he made her drink some. When her fever didn't abate, he immersed her in a cool stream. Knowing if he stopped she might die, he trudged on through the night.

Three days passed. He walked as a dead man, guilt riding on his every step. Elves moved into his line of sight before he realized they were saved. While the elves tended to Angela's wounds, Avery ate. He kissed her cheek before the others loaded her onto a wagon.

It was a race now. They were three days from Krikor. They ran the horses as fast as they dared … as fast as the terrain allowed.

CHAPTER 6

Krikor

W HERE IS THAT BEAUTIFUL MUSIC *coming from?* Angela opened her eyes. She didn't recognize her surroundings. *What has happened? Where is Alison? For that matter, where am I?*

Someone knocked. A head poked through the door. "Can I come in?"

When she recognized Serylda, it all came back to her. Avery had rescued her and told her she was the Alastrine Savior. As to the whereabouts of her sister, he hadn't known.

"Hi, Serylda. Come in. I'm so glad you survived." Her arm protested when she tried to move it.

"I feel the same about you, friend." Serylda entered and sat on the edge of Angela's bed. "If Derwyn hadn't found you two, you'd most certainly be dead by now."

"Did they find anything about my sister's whereabouts?"

"No, sorry." Serylda rose and strode to the window. She didn't see the tear Angela let fall down her cheek. The sun sent warm rays into the room. "We lost Hadek in the fight. Barak and Avery were the only ones unhurt." She held up her heavily bandaged left arm. "I broke this when one of Ahriman's men fell on top of me. We landed on a sharp rock. My arm broke our fall." She chuckled and returned to the bed. "But I got him before he could kill me."

"Good." Angela smiled back before becoming serious. "What happened to your disguise?"

"During the fight, my helmet fell off. I was identified right away. Barak's not sure what to do with me. I proved myself in the fight, so there's no reason for me to go home." She sat back down on the bed. "Angela, you've got to convince Barak I need to stay with you—go where you go. I feel responsible that you got hurt. I'm sorry."

"Wow." Angela shook her head and giggled. "There seems to be a lot of remorse going around. Even I wasn't immune to it. Avery and I promised each other we'd forgive ourselves." She laid a hand on Serylda's good arm. "It's your turn to do the same. No one is at fault. I could have as easily been captured at camp as I was out in the woods with Alison."

Just realizing what Serylda said earlier about the fight, she changed the subject. "Did you say we lost Hadek? How many others? Avery told me nothing of the battle." She let her hand drop to the bed. "What of Telek and Devlak?"

"Both are fine. They suffered wounds but are healing nicely. And Telek vowed to avenge Hadek's death. You knew he was Telek's brother-in-law?"

Angel shook her head. "That explains why they got along so well. I feel sorry for Telek. At least he knows what happened to Hadek. I wish I knew what happened to Alison. Is she still alive?"

There was another knock at the door. A young elfin girl entered. "I was told Angel was awake," she whispered.

"Yes, Ariel. She's probably hungry, too." She glanced at Angela who nodded agreement. "Ariel is Queen Kalika's personal aide. She was instructed to do whatever you wanted."

Angela smiled at the girl. "Thank you. All I need at present is a bath and some food."

"Yes, ma'am. I'll attend your bath water after bringing your meal." Ariel left, returning almost immediately with a tray of fruit and two glasses of juice. She placed the tray on the table near the bed and left again. Serylda helped herself to the food and handed Angela some, also.

The guitarist outside quit playing. "That was sure pretty. Do you think we could convince whoever that was to keep playing?"

Serylda laughed. "I wouldn't be surprised if that person would play especially for you." She leaned closer and in a secretive voice said, "It's Avery."

Angela's eyebrows rose in astonishment. Serylda nodded and sat back up.

The girls finished their meal and sipped the remainder of the juice. Angela felt better now that her stomach was full.

"When did I get here?"

"They brought you and Avery in, I think, ten days ago today."

Angela gasped. "Ten days?"

"You were at death's door." Serylda placed their empty glasses on the tray. "The elves are known for their healing powers. They saved your arm. In the shape it was, my people would have cut it off."

Angela looked at her bandaged right arm.

"I'd warn you though. They aren't sure if you'll gain total use of it. Your ability to use a bow may be gone."

"It was that bad?"

Serylda nodded.

"I won't miss that ability. I didn't like the thought of fighting." She felt an unusual sense of freedom. Perhaps she didn't have to combat Ahriman now.

"No, Angela. You are the Alastrine Savior. You have to defeat Ahriman. It's your destiny."

She sighed. *So much for that idea.*

A knock at the door brought the return of Ariel. She entered, followed by an elf dressed in white robes.

"The doctor," Serylda said. She rose. "I'll step outside. Yell if you need me." Angela nodded and watched her leave before turning her attention to the doctor.

"And now," the doctor began, "Ariel informed me you want a bath." His voice, soft and vibrant, gave her welcomed comfort. "We shall see. If I deem you well enough, she will take you to one. Don't get your hopes too high, but if after the bath you feel up to it, she will take you out for sunshine."

Angela listened to the doctor as she turned this way and that as he examined her. Shortly, he pronounced her fit enough to bathe and enjoy the sun afterward. Eager to get out of bed, Angela forgot her sore ankle. She bumped it against the bedpost in her haste to get up, and grimaced.

The doctor pointed at her ankle. "Let that make you more careful." He left the room, and Ariel returned to help her into another room. A steaming tub of water greeted them. With Ariel's help, Angela enjoyed her bath and the refreshing cleanliness afterward.

She donned a clean robe, and Ariel escorted her outdoors. The others of her company lounged under a huge apple tree a short walk from the building. Telek gave her his chair. The grass, a vibrant green, looked so soft and inviting. She wanted to sit on it and not a chair. No one allowed her the opportunity and insisted she sit on the provided chair. The company enjoyed the fresh air and each other's camaraderie. One of the men gathered some apples from the tree and passed them around.

"It's nice to see you up and about," Barak said. "You looked like Death's companion when I last saw you."

"To be honest, I felt like it too," she answered. Vaguely she remembered Barak visiting her when she was first brought in. She smiled at each in turn. It felt good sitting here among friends she never realized she had.

Turning serious, she faced Telek. "I heard about Hadek. I'm sorry. I'll do what I can to help. Both my parents died in a tornado a few years back. Well, back in my old time. Alison and I survived it. You will, too."

"Just defeat Ahriman. That will be enough."

Right. Everyone wanted her to defeat this Ahriman. But like her, Barak had his doubts, or so it seemed.

"We don't know if she is the one, Telek," Barak interrupted. "As soon as the doctor releases her, we'll go see Queen Kalika and learn the truth. In the meantime, we are to enjoy what the Elfin Nation has to offer."

"Yes," Avery agreed. "And we offer much. Our gardens are renowned for their soothing qualities. We have a vast herbal knowledge and put it to use by growing the herbs and spices that keep one healthy. Interspersed are flowers known for their scents and beauty."

"How long do you think we have before we meet the queen?" Serylda asked.

"According to the doctor, Angel's arm needs at least another two weeks to heal adequately before the bandage comes off. After that, we shall see."

"Play something for us," Telek interrupted. "Something to keep our minds off Ahriman and his threats." Avery nodded and picked up his guitar.

The days flew by quickly for Angela. Serylda stayed by her side continuously while Ariel helped her bathe and dress. The doctor stopped by every other day to check her wounds. They made sure no one tired Angela, allowing only so much time for each visitor. At night, Avery played his guitar under her window.

"You know he loves you," Serylda said one night. "You should let him know you feel the same."

"No." Angel chuckled once. "He's never told me that. In fact, since we've been here, he's hardly spoken to me. I think he feels guilty, and that's why you think he's in love. He's only trying to make me feel better. If he loves me, he'll have to tell me."

"I don't agree. He really loves you. I can see it in his eyes when he looks your way."

"As I said, I'll believe it when he tells me. But it is a nice dream, my dear friend." She patted Serylda's arm. "Let's get to sleep. We've a big day tomorrow. We're to meet Queen Kalika."

―⁓⁓⊙⦾⊙⦾⊙⊙⦾⊙⁓⁓―

The next day found Angela and the remainder of the company heading toward the royal house. The members of the company wore the same clothes they had traveled in. The elves had graciously cleaned and repaired them. The company looked as splendid as it had when they'd first started out on their journey over two months ago.

Along the way, Angela observed unusual things—walls made of growing trees and covered with thick briars stood everywhere. "How many years did it take the elves to train the vegetation to look like this?" she asked Serylda.

Serylda explained that the trees were living barriers to enemy forces, like castle walls. The elves lived in houses made of the living walls. They trained some of the branches into arches for doorways. Serylda didn't know what the elves did for the cold of winters when the vegetation was bare of their leaves.

Numerous gardens greeted their walk. Rows of vegetables and fruit trees grew so numerous she lost count. Grapevines draped over everything. She reached over and plucked some especially juicy-looking ones from a vine. Avery smiled at the ecstatic look she made after tasting one of the morsels.

There were many enclosures full of animals too. The fences were made of the briars and kept goats, pigs, and chickens safe. Yes, they ate more than just fruit.

She had asked for some kind of meat on the second day she was awake. The doctor denied her that, telling her they believed in lots of fruit for healing. She was allowed vegetables on her third day. Only yesterday was she allowed some meat, and not much. She had savored every bite.

The company walked up a small hill. The largest living fence of tangled briars and trees greeted them at the top. They had reached the royal house.

Two guards escorted them inside. The entrance resembled the medieval castle gates Angela had studied in sixth grade. They stood complete with portcullises, a drawbridge over a moat, and iron-studded, sturdy wooden doors.

Avery informed Angela that the elves had cleared out what structures had remained before training the vegetation into their "buildings." They had recycled what materials they needed to build the royal house and its grounds. An explanation of how they gained the knowledge to accomplish such a feat was left for another time.

Angela couldn't imagine a castle made of living things standing a chance in keeping the enemy out. Avery assured her this castle could, and had done so on numerous occasions. The entire Elfin Nation could escape to safety inside the walls in the event of an invasion.

The keep, or as the elves called it, the royal house, sat in the direct center of the huge wall of trees. Other buildings erected inside the outer wall housed temporary living quarters for the people in emergencies. The castle wall walk spanned the top of the buildings.

Once inside, the company was led to the king's chambers. Avery directed their attention to another door, behind which Queen Kalika's chambers lay. It stood facing the rising sun. The king's chambers served as the meeting place for the royal couple and the only entrance to the queen's chambers and sanctuary. Only a few souls ever set foot inside her rooms. Avery was one of the privileged few.

A sentry entered and stood at attention. "Make ready for the royal couple," he intoned.

The royal couple entered from the queen's chambers. They wore purple silk robes and crowns of gold and jewels. Behind them walked Ariel, holding the queen's train so it didn't drag. Avery marched up to the queen and gave her a kiss on her cheek.

"My son," the queen acknowledged. Her voice sounded so soft it was like the silk she wore.

Angela's eyes nearly fell out of their sockets. He was their son? Here stood the future king of the Elfin Nation. How ironic. She, who may be the Alastrine Savior, had to fall in love with him. How could she be worthy of such a person? Why did she do this to herself, becoming involved with things she found nearly impossible to get out of?

She discerned the similarities between Avery and Queen Kalika. His facial features mirrored hers. However, his blond hair was like that of his father, King Iomar Soren. Queen Kalika's hair shimmered like the stars and was just as dark as the midnight sky. It hung to her waist in flowing waves.

Avery walked back to the company and took hold of Angela's hand. He pulled her forward. "Mother, this is the woman you sent me to find. Her name is Angela Noland."

Angela, so nervous she trembled, bowed low, thinking that was the proper thing to do when one confronted royalty.

"Rise, my child," the queen said. Smiling, she held her hand out to Angela. "You are very much welcome in our kingdom."

Angela straightened and took the queen's hand. It was soft ... as soft as her voice. Angela smiled back at the queen, not sure what else to do; the queen seemed to render her speechless.

King Iomar suggested, "If the rest of you will follow me, we will retreat and find some refreshments. The queen has things to discuss with Angela." After kissing his consort on the cheek, he led the others out. Everyone bowed before leaving.

"And now, my child," Queen Kalika began, "we will retire to my chambers and talk." She drew Angela along through the door to her chambers and into another room off to the east.

The inner chamber was dark with windows draped in heavy curtains. A pedestal took center stage in the small room. Queen Kalika drew her near it.

"This is my special place. Only Iomar and Avery have been here." She sighed and let go of Angela's hand. "And I'm glad to be away from the formality out there. These robes aren't the most comfortable to wear. But before I can do anything about that, we need to discuss a few things. Here is where you will learn the answers to some of your questions." The queen took a deep breath and looked directly into Angela's eyes. "Are you the Alastrine Savior?" she continued. "Yes. I know you are the one we seek. I met you long ago. You will not remember the meeting. I was responsible for choosing you. I determined you were the best hope to aid us in our problem with Ahriman."

"I don't understand," Angela began. She moved to bring the pedestal between them. "Are you saying you brought me to this time? And what do you mean by 'your problem'?"

"I cannot answer your questions yet. Don't worry, you will find out in time. Trust me. You must travel to the Ancient Ones in the Great Crack." The queen smiled. "Excuse me, you will know it as the Grand Canyon." She removed a chain from around her neck. On the chain hung a crystal encased in gold. "This mineral carries a part of your DNA. It will show you and the world that you are the one chosen by the Ancient Ones, not your sister."

She moved around to Angela's side and placed the chain around her neck. The jewel began to glow and emit a little heat. Angela looked down at it, then at the queen.

"You may touch it. It is a part of you and will glow only for you, no one else."

"This material is not of the Earth, is it?" Angela realized suddenly, touching the stone.

"No, it isn't. It came from the Ancient Ones' home world. That is one of many reasons you must seek them out. Find them, Angel. Only they can give you the answers you seek. I have told you all I will. Any more information could prove dangerous for you at this time." She paused a moment. "From this time on, you will be known as Angel. Please accept this name."

Angel lowered her head and nodded.

"One more thing, my child. Trust Avery. He is there to aid you in your quest. I know you love him. I feel it. Do not be afraid to ask for his help or his love."

Angel knew great respect for the queen. She had one more question she had to ask, though. "Can you tell me ... do you know anything concerning my sister? I am worried for her."

The queen placed a gentle hand on her shoulder. "I can only say I am sorry. She will become a terrible burden for you in the days to come. Keep the good times you've both shared in your thoughts. They will comfort you."

Angel felt confused.

"Angel, I must insist that you let no one see the jewel, not even Avery. No one knows of its existence. If you decide to show it, use extreme caution. It can become a weapon against you."

Angel agreed. Queen Kalika led a very confused Angel out to the sunshine where the others waited patiently. What a day. After all the trouble of reaching Krikor, she had to retrace her steps and head back west. Only the Ancient Ones could tell her the answers—whoever they were.

King Iomar finished telling a story as the two women joined them. "My queen," he said and kissed her hand. "Is she the one?"

"Yes," the queen answered. She addressed the members of the company. "From this day on, Angela Noland shall be called Angel, the Alastrine Savior. Lord Barak, you and your dwarves are hereby charged to escort her to the Great Crack. There she is to seek out the Ancient Ones with Avery's help."

"We hear and obey, my lady." Barak rose to his feet and bowed low. The others followed suit.

"My son," the queen said, turning. "You are charged with the duty of being Angel's protector and adviser. Keep her safe on your journey."

"I understand, Mother." He bowed his head and glanced at Angel.

"When do we leave?" Serylda asked.

Barak turned to his sister. "Leave? You are going nowhere. You will stay safe here until Father sends you an escort home."

"Barak," Angel softly interrupted. "I want Serylda to come as my confidant and as a fellow woman on the trip. Also, I have a confession. I knew of Serylda's deception and have come to depend on her friendship in this strange land. She mentioned she fought well at the river. Are you going to deny her this chance to come along, especially since she's already proven herself?"

Barak looked to each member of the squad. Each one agreed with Angel. He sighed. "It looks as if I'm outnumbered. Serylda, you may accompany us. And I agree you proved yourself during the battle."

Serylda mouthed a thanks to Angel. "So," Serylda repeated, "when do we leave?"

"You begin your journey tomorrow morning," King Iomar said. "We will gather provisions. They should be ready by then."

"In the meantime," Queen Kalika added, "Ariel will take you to quarters here in the keep. You may rest if you so desire. Or take walks in our gardens. But, please don't leave the castle." The squad members thanked the royal couple.

Queen Kalika pulled Angel aside as the others left. "Remember my warning, Angel. Let no one see the stone. If Ahriman hears of its existence, he may figure a way to use it against you, then against the world. He knows of you and the threat you carry against him. He may try to kill you. Get to the Ancient Ones as fast as you can."

"How can he use a stone that glows only for me?"

"You will have to trust yourself to find the solution to that. In the meantime, you will learn most of your answers at the Great Crack. Avery will be with you all the way. He met the Ancient Ones when he was a child. Trust him."

Angel, frustrated, sighed and nodded. Trying to get the queen to say anything about the stone was a waste of time. Her answers lay with the Ancient Ones.

Outside the keep, Angel found the squad waiting for her. As she joined them, the royal couple reentered the keep. Ariel escorted the squad to a room on the south side of the building. Inside, they found mats covering the floor with two mats behind a fabric panel for the girls. They had the choice of either taking a nap or exploring the castle grounds. Everybody opted for the exploration.

Serylda grabbed Angel's hand and led her away from the men. "What did the queen say to you in that room?"

"Oh, I so wish I could tell you. She warned me to keep quiet about what was said in there. When I can tell you, I promise on our friendship, I will."

"Her demands don't surprise me. Everyone here seems to be keeping secrets." They reached a gigantic apple tree laden with fruit. Serylda plucked two ripe apples from a low branch. They sat in the shade and enjoyed their snack. The men chose to explore the castle's wall walk.

"I hate secrets," Angel said between bites. "I was told to trust Avery. But even he doesn't know what the queen and I talked about.

I'm not allowed to tell him, either." She rubbed her temples. "I'm so confused, Serylda. I'm ready to run away and hide."

"I sincerely hope you don't do that. You have to defeat Ahriman. I want to fight him so bad, I wish I could take your place."

Angel laughed. "I wish you could, too. I'm scared stiff."

Serylda snorted once. "That's a unique way of putting it."

The rest of the day went by quickly for the squad. They talked of nonsense to pass the time. Angel recounted her rescue and the badgercat she saw while Serylda told her of the battle she'd been in. When light began fading, they retired to their quarters. A hearty meal greeted them inside. Freshly cooked meat and vegetable stew filled the room with an inviting aroma. Fruit macerated in an alcoholic syrup ended the fine meal. Angel savored it as if it was her last.

After their meal the squad retired. A long day awaited them. Angel kept trying to think of ways to get out of the predicament she found herself in. As the hours passed and sleep eluded her, she started to doubt her abilities as well as the help the others had promised. And she kept asking herself, *Why me?*

CHAPTER 7

Hellos and Good-Byes

A NGEL AWOKE TO A KNOCK at the door. The royal couple entered, followed by an elfin male carrying a pitcher of water and Ariel carrying a tray of fruits and cheeses. The king and queen were dressed in tunics and breeches like their subjects, the purple silks left for formal occasions.

"The dawn breaks bright and cheerful," greeted the king. His warm smile mirrored his voice.

"Perhaps it is a favorable omen of success for your mission," the queen added. She gestured for the two who accompanied them to place their burdens on the table. "We bring you food to break your fast. We will talk after you have finished."

The royal couple took seats near the entrance and talked softly to each other. The squad ate quietly, not wanting to disturb them. Ariel left and returned with a bundle in her hands.

Avery strolled over to the male and hugged him. "Javas, my cousin. It's good to see you."

"Likewise, cousin," Javas answered. "I have just arrived back from Falconland and heard you were back too. Did I hear correctly? You were in a battle with a squad of Ahriman's men?"

"Yes," Avery said. He recounted the adventures he'd experienced since they'd last seen each other.

Angel used the time to study the newcomer. He stood as tall as Avery. His hair fell to his shoulders like that of all the elves. The color was darker than Avery's, a simple wheaten hue. She caught a glimpse of his eyes. Where Avery's eyes were a cobalt blue, Javas had emerald-green eyes. The men looked very much alike. If Avery had said "brother" instead of "cousin," Angel wouldn't have been surprised.

King Iomar clapped his hands. "Now that you have eaten, we have a few words to share. First, for those of you who are unfamiliar with him, this is Javas Ozuna. He will accompany you on your journey."

"We have no clothes befitting proud dwarven warriors," the queen said, "but I offer a few items suitable for Angel." She nodded at Ariel who handed over the bundle to Angel. The elfin girl bowed and left with the empty plate. "You will find what you need in that bundle. Since you lost the one you had, I've included a cloak, which is rainproof and suitable for desert travel."

Angel bowed low. "Thank you for your gracious offer, my lady."

"And now we turn to your journey," the king said. "Do you have a map?"

"Yes," Barak answered. Telek handed him one. "This is a recent copy, in fact. Made just before we left Jasper, sire." Barak unfolded it and laid it upon the table. Everyone gathered around.

Before anyone uttered a word, the door opened. An elfin male entered, whispered something to the king, and left. Everyone stood silent, glancing around questioningly.

A man over six feet in height and extremely thin strode in. His dirty-blond hair hung below his shoulders in a tangled mess. His beard and mustache weren't much better.

"Cornellius?" Avery stepped forward and clasped the man's hand. "What happened to you?"

Cornellius smiled. "Hello, old friend. I've been scouting up north at your father's request. I was trailing a group of Ahriman's men when I overheard one talking about the Alastrine Legend. One bragged to the other that his relative had captured the Savior and was taking her to Ahriman." He took a seat and continued. "I remember the legend saying the dwarves would know her first. The men said something about dwarves accompanying her east. So I figured I'd come here and find the truth. And help get her back if it's true."

"We welcome your help," Avery said for everyone assembled there. "By the way, I don't see Marlon. Where is he?"

Cornellius chuckled. "Where do you think? On the roof. You know how he is about enclosed places."

"Of course." Avery smiled and nodded.

On the roof? Angel wondered why anyone would sit on a roof. These people could be so strange.

"I want you to meet someone, Cornellius." Avery held out his hand toward Angel. "This is Angel, the Alastrine Savior. Ahriman's men have her twin sister."

Cornellius let out a sigh of relief. "Then all is not lost. A twin sister? Kind of confusing, eh?" He rose and placed his right hand over his heart. "I'm honored to meet you, Angel."

She smiled at his nod.

"Let's get back to business," the king said. "Probably the best route would be to stay a day's march north of the Red River, crossing these hills." He traced the route on the map as he spoke.

"A series of springs flows through there," Cornellius said, "if I'm not mistaken."

Angel remembered the springs near what had been Sulphur, Oklahoma. It had been her parents' favorite vacation spot. "Are the springs still cold?" she asked no one in particular.

"What?" Barak barked. "What did you say?"

"Never mind, friend Barak," the queen answered softly. She looked over at Angel and placed a finger to her lips, shaking her head at the same time. No one seemed to notice the exchange; they were studying the map. Barak turned back to the map after a moment of indecision.

Angel's spine tingled. The queen knew all about her and her time. Had the queen brought her forward somehow? If so, why hadn't she told the truth? And it seemed to her the queen didn't want Barak to wonder about Angel's question. *Is she worried about what he might think?* Angel inhaled deeply and then exhaled her breath. She wasn't going to get anything out of the queen. She forced her attention to the map and the talk around the table.

"We'd better skirt south of Amar," Evrak was saying.

Amar? Angel looked hard at the map. Of course, Evrak was pointing to the approximate area of Amarillo, Texas. "Why do we need to go around?" she asked.

"It is one of a handful of cities that escaped the Great Catastrophe," Telek answered. "Only evil abounds there. The perfect haven for thieves and cutthroats."

"From there, we can travel due west to the Great Crack," Barak added.

"You should reach it in about ten to twelve weeks," said the king.

"As long as we don't meet up with any of Ahriman's men," Serylda commented.

Angel frowned. "I have a question. I've noticed this mark in one other place, on the map at Jasper. What does it mean?" She pointed to the symbol over Krikor and another one over the Great Crack.

"It's the dwarven symbol for elf," Barak explained. "The elves originated from the Great Crack."

"Then the Ancient Ones ... ?"

"Are the very first elves," Queen Kalika said. "Our ancestors."

Angel looked around. Some of the squad members smiled. Others looked surprised that she hadn't known that fact.

Someone knocked at the door. Ariel entered, whispered in the king's ear, and left.

"Barak, your supplies are ready and waiting outside. We've provided you with food and water skins," the king said.

"We won't insult the Dwarven Nation by offering horses," the queen added. "But we ask that you take three to carry your supplies and make your burden lighter."

"I accept your gracious offer, my lady," Barak said and he bowed low.

"The morning is getting old, and you have a long road ahead. You should get started." King Iomar opened the door. All except the women followed him out.

"Now is the time to change into your traveling clothes, Angel," Queen Kalika said.

When the women emerged into the sunlight, Angel was dressed much like Avery and the other elves accompanying them—long pants with a drawstring waist covered by a loose-fitting shirt that hung halfway to her knees. The fabric was light and airy and gave her the sensation of being one with nature. The colors blended well with her surroundings. She felt the gold-encased crystal against her breast under the magical fabric. Her feet were shod in moccasins with the soles toughened for the long trek ahead. Queen Kalika warned her that it would take time for her feet to become accustomed to wearing them.

Finally, Ariel handed her a cloak and hat made of the same fabric as her shirt and pants. They would be a nice addition in the cool desert nights.

Angel watched as a falcon landed upon Cornellius's arm at his whistle. "Meet Marlon, Angel."

"Ah, then, Marlon is a bird?"

Cornellius nodded.

"I was having a hard time imagining someone wanting to be up on a roof."

Everyone laughed.

"Do you not hood him?" Angel asked.

"We feel that is mean to the bird. I know it was done in the past. We train them to stay with one person for life. It is better for both man and bird, we think."

Everyone nodded at Cornellius's statement. Angel smiled.

"Good luck, my son." The queen hugged Avery. "Our thoughts go with you."

"Get Angel safely to the Ancient Ones," the king added, clasping Avery's arms. Then, holding his arms wide, he addressed the rest of the squad. "May the sun shine in blessing upon your journey."

The squad as one bowed low to the royal couple. Angel thought about each of the members of the squad as the twelve turned and began their long journey to the Great Crack. The dwarves in the squad consisted of Barak Blackstone and his sister Serylda. Telek Ironbar offered to cook. Evrak Scarstone, Fynbar Smithy, and Kendrik Graybeard, three of those who survived the skirmish at the Red River, finished out the dwarves.

There were four elves. Avery Soren was joined by his cousin, Javas Ozuna. The other two were twins, Derwyn and Merwyn Lunn. Angel couldn't tell them apart even though Avery had no trouble whatsoever.

Only one man accompanied them. From Damar in Falconland, Cornellius Fraomar with his pet falcon, Marlon, would serve as the squad's hunters. They were charged with supplying the squad with fresh meat at least once a day.

Barak led, followed by Avery, Angel, and Serylda. Javas and the others were next with Telek bringing up the rear. Devlak and the remaining nine dwarves were to remain with the elves for three more days of recuperation. Afterward they were to travel to Boman and rally the dwarves that lived there. The Bomani dwarves would travel to Attor, gathering a company of elves on the way back through Krikor. If all went as planned, the squad would meet at Ahriman's evil fortress by the middle of August.

I hope, Angel thought.

CHAPTER 8

Niedra

T HE SQUAD HAD BEEN ON the move since morning with no breaks. Noontime had come and gone. Angel couldn't see what Barak's hurry was. At the rate they were traveling, she'd be so tired that she'd be useless once they reached the Great Crack. And it was just the first day.

To take her mind off Barak, she took more notice of her surroundings. They were in the Ozark Mountains. The tips of the hills peeked above the fog that shrouded the land. It was strenuous walking, and it reminded her of home.

She was painfully aware of her homesickness. Ah, to be home, to wake up and realize this was all a dream. It would be nice to just flip a switch again or get in a car and drive to their destination. But she knew better. Too many things had happened to her already. She wasn't Dorothy of Oz. She was Angel in a future wrought with perils she never dreamed of. A tear slid down her cheek. She turned her head so no one would see her cry and stepped on a stone.

Yes, her feet hurt too. *It's going to take some time to get used to wearing moccasins,* she thought, remembering what the queen had told her. *And it hasn't been a full day yet. Almost, but not quite.* She felt every stone and every twig. Her feet seemed like magnets to all obstacles.

Barak called a halt an hour later. Angel promptly sat and rubbed her ankles. She wondered why Barak had waited so long before stopping. She felt it must be past suppertime.

Serylda joined her and smiled. "Tired?"

"Only my feet." Angel returned her friend's smile. Reluctantly she rose and helped Serylda erect their tent. This time the men preferred to sleep out in the open. No tents for them.

Cornellius and Marlon left to hunt. Javas left also, taking a different route. He came back with tubers. Telek sent Fynbar and Kendrik for wood while he busied himself with preparing the fire pit. In no time at all, a fire roared in the newly formed pit. Shortly after Cornellius returned with two squirrels, a stew enhanced with the meat simmered over the fire. Everyone gathered around and savored the aroma coming from the cooking food.

While they waited, Barak set up guard duty tours, having twelve people to work with. (Angel had insisted she take a turn despite everyone's disagreement in the matter.) He chose three, three-hour tours of guard duty. And since Angel was the least experienced, she received third-tour camp watch. It was her duty to awaken the squad as each new day began. Everyone agreed with the arrangement, and they would keep the order throughout their journey. Having decided on the guard tours, everyone went about his or her business while waiting on supper.

Secretly, Angel was relieved, but she knew why Barak had chosen the position of camp watch for her. If there was trouble, she'd be near enough to Avery and Barak for help, the two most experienced members of the squad.

She was glad for a second reason. Her right arm wasn't yet strong enough to pull a bow taut. And she wasn't confident enough in her ability to use a knife in combat, her only remaining option. She felt worse off now than when she'd started on this journey back in March. And that seemed such a long time ago.

She sat near the tent, her legs crossed underneath her. She looked around for Serylda and spotted her north of camp working with a quarterstaff. Curiosity getting the better of her, she got up and joined her friend.

"Is that hard to learn?" Angel asked. "Can you teach me how to use that?"

Serylda stopped twirling the weapon. "Sure." She looked over at the campfire surrounded by the men not on duty. "But, I should talk to Barak first … get his approval." She leaned the staff against a nearby tree and left to talk to her brother.

Angel stayed where she was. She looked over the weapon, being careful not to touch it. It was about a foot taller than she was. A piece of leather covered one end and made a bulge. The other end was sharpened to a dull point. Angel could well imagine the damage such a weapon could inflict with an expert wielding it.

If Barak didn't allow her to learn to use such a weapon, she promised herself to put up such a fuss he'd relent just to shut her up. He had to see the benefits. It might depend on how fast she learned. *Fast enough*, she thought with determination.

Serylda returned, a smile on her face. "I'm not surprised. He approved. He wondered when we'd ask him. But he did say he'd test you when he wished and as many times as he wished." She leaned closer to Angel. "Between you and me, I think he's too cautious at times."

"And demanding," Angel added. The girls laughed loudly. The men looked at them in wonder.

Angel's training began with learning the correct way to hold the staff, whether in battle or not. It took all of five minutes. To Angel, it wasn't much different than swordplay. She had helped Alison with her sword training, serving as her guinea pig. Of course they had used wooden swords instead of steel swords. Barak had been sure of that.

Serylda marked a tree and showed Angel how to stab it with the butt end. Angel did as shown, staying conscious of her stance. It would be well to learn correctly now rather than to have to relearn later. Ten minutes later, Serylda called a halt.

"You learn fast. At this rate, you'll be battle ready in, I'd say, about two weeks. Possibly sooner."

"You think so?" Angel sat down and leaned against the tree she had used as her "enemy." The quarterstaff lay on the ground next to her. "Tell me about some of the history of this weapon, Serylda." She patted the staff for emphasis.

"It's a very old, very efficient weapon. All dwarves know how to fight with one by the age of eight. It is considered a female weapon of choice."

"Their weapon of choice?"

"We can choose what weapon we want. The problem is, most women don't have the strength to use anything except this."

"And males know its use too?"

"Yes."

"So, axes and swords are male weapons?"

"Yes."

"Does it cause tension among your people for them to know you prefer a male weapon at times?"

"No, because I'm the dwarflord's daughter." Serylda smiled. "And because Barak taught me in secrecy, earlier than what was allowed. I was determined to learn how to use an ax, so I took his to practice. He found me out after I came back with a nasty cut on my leg. Since I tried to hide it and doctor the cut myself, I have a nice scar to remind me of my foolishness." She peered at the ground. "Anyway, Barak saw how determined I was, bandaged my cut properly, and began training me."

"So you are truly a battle maid."

"Yes," Serylda said. "And here's something ironic. My name literally means 'battle maid.'" They laughed.

The girls relaxed and enjoyed their camaraderie away from the men. Darkness had settled over the camp. The stars came out in brilliant twinkling masses. There was no moon that night. It was the first day of the new phase. Angel heard footfalls coming from the direction of the fire.

"Excuse me, but Master Barak bid me to inform you supper is ready."

"Thank you," Angel said, not remembering the dwarf's name. The girls rose, and Angel stooped to retrieve the staff.

"Lead, Kendrik," Serylda said. "We'll follow."

After supper, everyone retired. The food was left near the fire to stay warm for the three on perimeter watch. Angel smeared insect cream over her exposed skin, compliments of Serylda, and lay down on her bedroll. The cream proved very effective. She was tired after the day's march in her new shoes and the training with the quarterstaff.

No sooner had she fallen asleep when someone was shaking her awake.

"What?" she asked, irritated.

"Your watch is up," said a tired Serylda. She fell onto her bedroll.

"Oh, yeah," Angel reflected. "Sorry." She rose and stretched the sleep from her limbs. It felt a touch nippy, so she wrapped her cloak about her shoulders. Serylda was snoring, having fallen asleep as soon as her head touched her bedroll. Angel shook her head in amazement. What would her dwarf friend have been like in her time?

Strapping on her knife and grabbing Serylda's quarterstaff, she left the tent. Silently she thanked Serylda for giving her permission earlier to borrow it. Avery stood near the fire. Six snoring dwarves and elves encircled them.

"All seems quiet," she whispered in greeting.

"So far," Avery answered. "I'm not tired. Why don't you go back to bed? I'll take your watch."

"No. I insist on taking my fair share of the duties like everyone else. But, thanks anyway." She stirred the fire and watched a few firebrands escape.

Avery put another log on the fire. "We have little to worry about yet," he said. "We're too close to Krikor for Ahriman's men to attempt an ambush. I noticed you limping earlier today, so why don't you take my offer and go back to sleep?"

"I really appreciate it, Avery. But I am still a part of this squad and will do my share." She stifled a yawn.

He smiled. "Even though you are tired?"

"Yes, even though I'm tired." She stretched again and took a deep breath. "I need to do my share. Or I'll feel inadequate and not really a part of this expedition."

She began her rounds, the quarterstaff in her hands. Avery accompanied her, not ready to retire.

Since he walked with her, she decided to ask him a question. "Do you know what I'm to do when I meet Ahriman?"

"No. We hope the Ancient Ones can tell you."

She pinched her lower lip between thumb and finger a moment. "That's not very helpful. What if we don't find them? How do I defeat a being who's immortal? Especially since none of you seem to be able to do this either. How can I, a simple girl, do this thing? It scares me to think about it."

"Don't criticize yourself, Angel. You're worth more than you know." They had returned to the fire's warmth. "You will feel more able to do what you're destined for after you become proficient with the staff and meet with the Ancient Ones. Trust me on that."

"Okay. But I have one more question, please." At his nod, she continued. "Who are the Ancient Ones?"

He smiled. "My ancestors."

She studied him hard. "You know how I got here, don't you?"

He shook his head. "I'm sorry, but I don't. I asked my mother, but she wouldn't tell me. She said the answer lies at the Great Crack. We have to have faith in her words and know we'll find the answers there. She wouldn't relent." Avery placed a hand on her shoulder. "Don't worry. All will turn out fine."

"But what if it doesn't? What if I fail? What then?"

"Let's worry about that if it happens and not before, okay?" He let his hand drop.

She stared at the fire a moment and listened to its crackle. Turning back, she agreed. "Well, you may as well get some sleep. I'll cry out if I need anything."

He nodded his head once and retired. His bedroll lay farthest from the fire. Soon she knew he slept although she wasn't sure how. He didn't snore. She looked at the sleeping men around her. Funny, only the dwarves were snoring. *Do I snore? I hope not.*

Idle thoughts ran through her mind during her tour. She made rounds when she felt sleep creeping up on her. Stubbornly, she kept her thoughts from Ahriman, Alison, and her own predicament, taking Avery's suggestion of not worrying to heart. Even so, her thoughts kept returning to her twin. She prayed Alison was still alive. Any other thought was too much for her.

The eastern sky began to lighten when Barak rose from his bedroll. That was one she didn't have to rouse. She stirred the fire and put a couple of logs on to strengthen the flames for the coming morning.

Picking up a big bowl and a pot, Barak nodded in her direction and ambled toward a nearby creek. When he returned, the dishes were filled with water. He placed them on the fire and rummaged through his pack. He brought out a packet of tealeaves and added some to the water in the pot and retrieved the bowl. After washing his face, he tossed the used water into the brush. He picked up two cups from near the fire and poured tea into each. Without a word he offered one to Angel. She accepted it with a nod.

The sky had lightened considerably by then. Everyone was stirring. Even Serylda had emerged from the tent. Angel didn't have to rouse any of them. An hour later the squad was once more on their way. Having walked the perimeter several times during her tour, Angel's feet felt better able to handle the day's trek. They caused her no trouble, and she enjoyed the morning.

———〜vv•o੦⌒o୧๏੦ᴿ੦⌒o⌒੦•o•vv———

The squad had been traveling for a week now. The afternoon was hot and sultry. They were still heading in a westerly direction. Though Angel occasionally caught glimpses of city ruins in the distance as they traveled, she had no idea where they were. Forested areas thick with briars surrounded them. At times, it was so thick they had to cut a path through just to keep moving.

Barak pushed them hard. Angel learned from Serylda that they were nearing an ancient thoroughfare. From Barak's map, Angel knew they had to be in Oklahoma of "her time." The squad had traveled some two hundred miles since leaving Krikor. That should put them near what she remembered as I-35. Perhaps near Ardmore?

Barak acted as if he wasn't going to stop for some time yet. She turned to Serylda. At least talking to her friend took the day's heat off her mind. "Tell me about Falconland." Angel watched the falcon on Cornellius's shoulder. Marlon's eyes darted back and forth continuously, perhaps looking for a mouse or other such critter.

"Well," Serylda began, "it's a country south and east of Krikor, near the ocean and in a swampy region. I can show you on one of Barak's maps later, if you like. The men there train falcons to hunt. It's easier than trekking through bogs and marshes full of snakes, among other deadly creatures."

"What kind of cities are there?"

"There's only one, Damar. It's on an island in the center of the swamp, one of the few dry places there. There are other villages scattered throughout. But they are on tiny islets, or wherever they can build."

The squad stopped as briars blocked their way. Angel found a fallen tree, and the girls sat on the trunk to await the barrier's removal.

"It makes for a great place to live," Serylda continued, "if you don't mind living on islets. It's easily defended according to the people, and nearly impregnable. Ahriman would have a hard time conquering the Falconlanders."

They started moving again.

"Tell me a little about your home, Angel." Serylda grinned. "I'm very curious."

"Well, it's nothing like this," Angel said. She looked up at the towering trees. The terrain was leveling out, not as hilly. They sidestepped a few bushes.

What should she tell her? How does a person explain electricity or vehicles to one who's never seen such things? And what about computers and airplanes?

"Serylda, I'm from the past. I'm guessing about two thousand years."

"Yes, I know that. In fact everyone does. It's part of the legend."

"Really?" Angel's eyebrows rose. "Okay. In my time, we had learned how to harness lightning. We learned how to bring it inside to light our homes at night safely. I so miss it at times too. This time is like the Dark Ages to me."

"Dark Ages?"

Suddenly Angel stopped and held up her right hand. Instinct took over. She strongly sensed something near.

"What?" Serylda asked. Everyone stopped and turned at her question.

"Shh," Angel whispered. A subtle heat emanated from the vicinity of her heart. She drew her left hand to her breast. *It's the crystal!* she realized.

What is it telling me? Is it glowing as Queen Kalika told me it would? Are we in danger? She didn't feel threatened. The experience felt more animalistic … alien. A sense of curiosity intermingled with apprehension, and fear touched her nerves. And for some reason, it felt familiar. A thought popped into her head. "Avery?" She kept her voice low and gentle but loud enough for Avery to hear her. "Where did you rescue me? Is it nearby?"

"As a matter of fact, yes. It's less than a half a day's walk south of here. Why? Do you sense danger?"

"Not exactly. More like a curiosity. I can't explain any better than that." She faced the squad. "Please, everyone, stand still. I think we have a visitor, and I don't want to frighten it."

She turned toward the bushes where the source of the emotions seemed to emanate. She took a few steps closer and saw the animal.

The face of a badgercat stared out at her. Its iridescent orange eyes glowed like jewels.

"Hello, there," she said softly.

"Angel," Barak interrupted, "move away slowly. That's a badgercat." His ax was in his hands. He stood battle ready. The other dwarves had followed his lead. Even Serylda held her staff at the ready. But all the elves took their cue from Avery who just stood still.

Angel stole a glance in Barak's direction. "I know. Please, I asked you to keep still." She shifted her glance back to the animal. "It won't harm anyone as long as everybody obeys me."

"And how in the world would you know that?"

She ignored Barak. Concentrating on the cat, she held out her right hand, palm down. From the corner of her eye, she saw Barak take a step forward. Avery placed a hand on the dwarf's shoulder and shook his head.

The animal came out of its hiding place and, oh so gently, touched Angel's hand with its nose. At that exact moment, the cat's thoughts flooded her mind.

The crystal felt hot against her breast. The animal's thoughts washed over her like a tidal wave. *The crystal must be some kind of transceiver. I know I am feeling the badgercat's true thoughts.*

She saw a vast whirlwind descend from the clouds followed by images of buildings, some standing, some collapsed. Images of Avery and herself imprinted onto her senses. The animal had recognized them from the ancient city where Avery had rescued her. A sense of animalistic maternal protectiveness flooded through her.

Amazing, she thought. She fell back, sitting on the ground and breaking physical contact with the animal. The thoughts that flooded her before were still there but much muted.

"Angel?" A note of anxiety crept into Avery's voice. The cat growled, low pitched and soft.

"It's okay," she answered. She tried sending feelings of well-being to the cat. She hoped it would work. It stopped growling and began to purr. "It wants to protect me. I truly believe it would lay down its life for me."

"How, may I ask, do you know that?" Barak still stood battle ready, feet spread apart, ax in his hands, his left hand near the blade and his right gripping the handle.

"I just do." She stood and faced the squad, being careful to place herself between them and the cat. "Please, put away your weapons."

No one did. The dwarves looked at Barak instead.

"Now!" Angel demanded. Her voice, hard and low, commanded obedience. "No one will come to harm, or harm this animal, as long as I am near. Understand?"

Everyone obeyed. Everyone, that is except Barak.

"Barak, I'm deadly serious." Her hands rested on her hips. "You will not harm this animal. Put your ax away. Now."

Stubborn to the end, he ignored her demands. "You have no idea the harm this animal is capable of. They can rip a man to shreds in a matter of minutes. It is a very painful death, Angel. I've witnessed it."

"I know that, Barak. But, I also know this animal's feelings. It will kill you to protect me if it feels you're threatening me." She took a step toward Barak. The cat stopped purring and stared at him. "Please, Barak." She got no response. *Stubborn dwarf.*

"Okay, let me put this in another way. I feel protective toward this animal. Do you wish us to fight, Barak, you and me?" Her heart pounded. She was taking a big risk taunting the dwarf. She needed him to back down.

He looked at the cat, then back at her. "Fine. I'll abide with your demands for now. But, be warned, Angel. If that animal so much as threatens one of my men, I *will* kill it." He patted his ax for emphasis and replaced it on his back. "I hope you understand me clearly."

She felt the badgercat's fear mingled with her own. "Don't worry, Barak. She has no intention of harming anyone in this squad." *How can my voice sound so calm when I'm quaking with trepidation?* She turned her back to Barak, stopped, and spun back around. "Oh, and that includes you. So if you stay out of her way, she'll stay out of yours."

She spun back toward the animal. It sat on its haunches. Her heart slowed to normal. "You need a name, my feline companion." She petted the cat. "How about *Niedra,* after a dear friend of mine?" The cat purred loudly in response.

Angel stood and faced the squad. Holding out her hand, she said, "I'd like to introduce you all to Niedra, my mascot and protector. And your protector, as well, may I add."

"Amazing," Javas said. "Has anyone ever heard of such a thing? A badgercat befriending a human?"

"I've never heard of it," Avery answered. "I wonder why it took to us. Angel, do you have any idea as to why?"

"It recognized us—you and me, Avery. It's the same one we saw after you rescued me." She regarded the cat a moment longer and then joined the others. The cat rose and followed her. The journey resumed with one more member.

Everyone gave Angel and Niedra a wide berth. Shortly, Serylda joined Angel and the cat, overcoming her fear. But she kept Angel between her and the badgercat to be safe.

"Do you think it would let me pet it?" Serylda asked. "It's been a fantasy of mine, to have a badgercat loyal only to me. And don't let my brother worry you. He witnessed three of his men being torn to shreds by a pack of them. He escaped only because there were three cats and four men, and he happened to be the farthest away."

"Thanks, that explains a lot." Angel squeezed her friend's hand. "The answer to your question is, yes, I think she'll let you touch her. But, not just yet. When Niedra's more comfortable around everyone, she will then." She petted the cat for reassurance, without stooping. It came to her shoulder while on all four feet. There was no bending to reach this animal!

"You sure surprised me back there." Serylda's voice cut into her musings.

"Oh? How so?"

"The way you stood up to my brother took courage. You're the only female I know of to have done so and got away with it. What Barak says is usually taken as law, unless our father deems different. Which is seldom nowadays."

"To be honest, Serylda," Angel confided, "I was as afraid of him as Niedra was of him at first. Probably more so. Please don't tell him what I said. I just wanted to make sure no one harmed Niedra. He seemed determined to do so."

Serylda glanced down at Niedra. "That animal was afraid? That's hard to believe."

"Why?"

Serylda shrugged. "I don't know. I just thought they were never afraid due to their aggressive nature."

Angel smiled. "All living things can harbor fear, my friend. It's not assigned only to humans, dwarves, and elves."

They chuckled in good humor. The cat purred alongside them.

Five miles later, Barak called a halt. Angel was thankful. Her feet were numb. He chose a place on the opposite side of the stream from the spot where they had camped the last time they were near this part of the Red River.

The cat had never left Angel's side during their trek. After the squad stopped, the animal tensed up. Angel looked down to see her leap into the brush on her left. She smiled as it disappeared.

"Wow," Serylda said, alarm in her voice. "Where did it go in such a hurry?"

"What?" Barak barked. "Where's that cat?" He unsheathed his axe. All others just glanced around.

"Put your weapon away, Barak. Niedra's only hungry, like the rest of us. She went hunting." The badgercat returned, holding in its mouth the biggest rodent Angel had ever put eyes to. "See?" Niedra found a shady tree to lie under and began eating. The crunch of bones as it ate made Angel shudder.

"Sounds vicious," Serylda commented. The others turned away and started setting up camp.

Angel nodded. "At least *she's* eating." Her stomach growled at her words, and the girls laughed.

The sun sank below the horizon. The light began to fade; total darkness was less than an hour away. Cornellius took his bird to hunt while Telek concentrated on the fire. Javas just disappeared. One moment he was with them, the next moment he was gone. Avery didn't seem concerned, so she didn't worry either. Camp stood ready, and watch was set as before. Niedra, finished with her light meal, licked her paws, and watched Angel as she helped gather wood.

Cornellius returned with four freshly dressed rabbits. Javas, close behind, carried tubers and wild onions he'd found in the forest. While Cornellius and Telek boned the meat, Javas chopped the vegetables for the stew.

"Angel, do you think your cat would like some bones?" Telek held up a handful, his eyebrows raised.

"Let's see."

She offered them to the cat. Being very dainty, Niedra chose one of the largest bones and ignored the rest. She ambled over to the front of the girls' tent and plopped down. Angel sensed the animal's contentment as it gnawed at the bone.

She handed the rest of the bones back to Telek and joined the others sitting around the fire. Telek threw the bones far into the scrub, away from camp. He stepped up to the fire and stirred the stew, smiling at Angel. She smiled back. The stew smelled delicious. Why did camping always make food taste and smell so good?

The moon showed her face in a cloudless sky. The stars popped out in multitudes. A slight breeze ruffled hair and cooled bodies. Sighs were made all around. The night came alive with insects buzzing and crickets chirping and frogs croaking.

"I've been thinking about the badgercat." Javas broke the silence. "Do you think it knows of Angel's importance?"

"Possibly," Avery responded. "That would answer a lot of questions."

"Like how some animals know when bad weather is coming or an earthquake is about to happen?" asked Kendrik Graybeard, the short, blond dwarf.

"Angel, has that cat told you anything of itself?" Barak asked. "For example, how old is it? Has it had kittens? Can it sense danger?"

Angel was relieved to hear only curiosity from Barak's questions. She closed her eyes and concentrated upon Niedra. Nothing. She walked over to the cat and laid a hand on the animal's head. She posed Barak's query by forming an image of kittens.

No one was prepared for the anguished wail that came from the cat's throat. Some crouched low, while others glanced about apprehensively. All drew weapons.

"What's wrong with it?" Avery shouted.

Angel put her arms around the animal's huge head. It quieted down as suddenly as it had begun its cry. She looked up at Avery, and tears streamed down her cheeks. "She lost her two babies in that storm. Her first litter, newly born."

Serylda went over to the cat, sympathy in her eyes. The badgercat mewed. Courageously, she held out her hand as Angel had done, palm down. "Poor thing," she cooed. "Such a tragedy."

"Serylda!" Barak's voice barely carried to them, but it held such terror both girls spun. "What are you doing? Back away. Slowly."

"Easy, Barak," Angel said normally. "Niedra wouldn't hurt her." Niedra licked Serylda's hand. "See? She knows when someone is sympathetic. As a matter of fact, none of you need worry about her hurting you. She's adopted all of you. She'd protect each one as if you were me. Even you, Barak."

"I'm still not sure," he responded. "After what I saw as a youth, it's going to take more than your word for me to feel comfortable around her."

"Don't worry. Niedra understands your apprehension. She harbors the same toward you, though she'd kill to protect you."

Barak's stance didn't waver. Angel scowled at him and then turned to Serylda. "You will not come near Niedra unless I am there, okay?"

"Yeah," Serylda agreed, and rose. "Will that suit you, brother?"

Still scowling, Barak conceded. "It does not, but I will accept those terms." He sat down and added, "For now."

Telek, standing by the fire, cleared his throat and said, "If everyone has settled down now, supper is ready."

"Thank you," Barak said. "But I still have a question I want answered. Can it sense danger?"

Angel touched the cat's head. It growled low in its throat. Serylda backed off slowly and resumed her seat next to Barak.

Angel stood. "Yes. Niedra knows when danger threatens. It first saw me with Ahriman's men and knew they were evil. So, she followed us. When Galth attacked me, she could do nothing since she was in labor at that time. Are you satisfied now?"

Not waiting for an answer, Angel grabbed a bowl and spooned herself some stew. Ignoring everyone, she joined the badgercat in front of the tent. As she relaxed, she ate and listened in on the squad's conversations.

Javas was speaking. "Is there anything in the dwarven histories about Angel talking to animals like this?"

Barak took a big bite of his stew before answering. "I've heard of no such thing. But Devlak was our historian. He knows more than me."

"What about your people, Cornellius?" Javas took a bite of his stew.

Cornellius shook his head and swallowed. "Sorry."

It grew quiet as they all concentrated on their meals. With supper finished and enough left over for the ones on first watch, the squad worked quietly together and cleaned up. Angel returned to the cat after the work was finished, having done her fair share.

The elves ambled away from the rest and talked quietly among themselves. Serylda retrieved the jar of insect repellent from Telek and joined Angel and the cat.

"The bugs will be swarming soon," she said as she sat next to Angel.

"Thanks," Angel replied. And with a vengeance, an inch-long mosquito landed on her arm, giving her a nasty bite. She made an awful mess squishing the annoying bug. To top it off, she endured two more bites before getting the cream spread on her exposed skin.

"It's been a long day. I think I'll retire early." Angel yawned as she entered the tent.

"I'll join you later," Serylda responded. She rose and joined her brother next to the fire.

Angel entered the tent and curled up in her bedroll. She was wide awake. She mulled over the day's events, especially the events with the badgercat, Niedra.

She had never bonded with an animal like she had done today. And it had been so easy, which scared her a bit. Her thoughts turned to those huge claws. She had felt no fear around the cat. Niedra would die protecting her. She knew that with confidence. *Why?* That was something she didn't understand.

And why couldn't I have stayed in my own time? Why me? Alison is the stronger of us. A tear ran down her cheek. She wanted to go home to her century with her sister. Angel cried herself to sleep, knowing the badgercat kept vigilant watch over the tent.

CHAPTER 9

Stormy

T HE AIR WAS DECIDEDLY HOTTER, and the terrain was drier. Mesquite bushes and briars abounded. The trees became scarce. If Angel's reckoning was right, it was May 24, and they were due south of Amarillo, Texas. *Or, as this time calls it, Amar,* she reminded herself.

They hadn't seen any sign of Ahriman or his men. Everyone kept talking about the impending doom she was supposed to prevent. And on top of that, Angel was tired. It had been a long day. Their water supply was becoming harder to replenish the farther west they traveled. Today, they hadn't come across one stream, but the others didn't seem too worried.

She felt uneasy as she helped set up the tent. A feeling of anger swept over her when she glanced at Serylda. She gasped. Where did that come from? She wasn't angry at anyone. Was she sensing Serylda's feelings?

True, Barak and Serylda had had a heated argument earlier in the day. But, how was she picking up that anger? She looked over at Barak and felt frustration and displeasure. *Barak's feelings? How?*

Angel kept her eyes glued to the ground and concentrated on her own feelings. She was aware of the apprehension she harbored the closer they got to the Great Crack. Those feelings of anger and displeasure were definitely not hers. So how was she receiving them?

A thought entered her mind. The Ancient Ones might be responsible. Especially if it was they who had brought her sister and her here to this time.

The badgercat padded up to her. Angel sensed concern from her. When the tent was up, Serylda went off to one side and began polishing her weapons. Angel patted the big cat's head, sat down, and leaned against a tree. Niedra joined her, lounging in the grass.

It had started with Niedra, she realized. Before, she had to touch the animal to feel its thoughts. This time, she had sensed its concern before she touched it. She wondered if Avery could explain it. It was worth asking him.

Rising, she instinctively clutched at the crystal inside her tunic. What was this? The crystal was warm. Her eyes fastened upon Cornellius. He was petting and talking to his bird. Determination invaded her thoughts. At the same instant, the crystal grew warmer.

It had to be the crystal doing this to her. She sighed. At least she wasn't going crazy. But how was this crystal projecting alien thoughts into her mind? She needed to talk to Avery. After all, it was his mother who had given her the stone.

She stopped. Queen Kalika had warned her not to let anyone know of it. How could she ask for Avery's advice then? What a dilemma.

She returned to the cat and sat back down against the tree. Niedra dozed next to her. She closed her eyes and concentrated on the animal. Nothing. She opened her eyes and stared at Niedra. The cat was dreaming of chasing some kind of creature.

Interesting. It seemed she needed to be looking at whatever or whomever in order to hear any thoughts. That gave her another problem. Every time she looked at one of her comrades, she'd be reading his or her innermost feelings. It had happened with Serylda, Barak, and Cornellius already.

She took a deep breath, her mind made up. Now was the time. No matter what Queen Kalika had told her, she needed Avery's help. For that, he had to learn of the crystal. So, why didn't she get up and go to him? Fear. That was it. She was afraid.

"Are you okay?"

She jumped and looked up. Avery's concern invaded her brain. Looking at his boots, she answered, "I don't know." Fear or no, she needed his help. "Can we go somewhere more private to talk?"

"Sure." He offered his hand to help her to her feet.

"No, don't touch me, please. I'll explain in a moment. Let's just go." She rose and followed him while keeping her eyes averted from him and on the ground.

He led her about a hundred paces from camp. It was far enough away for their conversation yet near enough to yell if help was needed.

Avery sat on a fallen log. "Now, what's wrong? I sense confusion and a little fear from you."

She rubbed her face and clasped her hands in her lap. "I hear thoughts that aren't my own. I've even heard some of the thoughts of members of the squad." Her words became rushed. She was afraid that, if she stopped now, her courage would fail. "I'm afraid to touch or even look at anyone now. Since you have the ability to feel others' emotions, I'm hoping you can help."

"When did this start?"

"It started with the cat. Before, I had to touch it to hear its thoughts. Now all I have to do is look at it. It happens whenever I look at anyone. I've caught Serylda's, Barak's, and Cornellius's thoughts so far. What's wrong with me?"

He leaned forward, clasped his hands together, and placed his elbows on his knees. "I've never heard of anyone developing such a talent outside the Elfin Nation. And only a few of us are adept at it. We who are born with the ability learn how to control it as we grow." He sat up and glanced at her. "Did my mother say anything concerning this?"

"No." She hesitated and then drew out the crystal. "She gave me this and warned me not to let anyone see it, including you. She said to keep it secret. But, I need help. I trust you the most." She took a deep breath and continued. "She told me it belonged to me. It showed I was the chosen one. It gets warm when I hear thoughts, Avery." She removed the crystal from her neck and handed it to him, being careful not to touch him. "Do you have any clue as to what it is?"

"It looks like an ordinary crystal to me, Angel. I've got an idea, though. Look at me and tell me if you can sense anything."

"I'm afraid to," she confessed. Her eyes stayed on the ground.

"Don't worry, Angel. I have the discipline to shield my mind enough to ease your discomfort. I will allow only what I want you to hear. I want to see if it's the crystal doing this or if it's something entirely different."

She trusted him and did as he asked. Nothing. She concentrated harder. "I sense nothing," she said, comforted.

"Okay. Take the crystal back, and let's try this again. And don't be afraid."

With the crystal back around her neck, once more she did as he asked.

Do you hear my thoughts?

"Yes!" She averted her eyes and smiled with relief. "Then it is the crystal, and I'm not going crazy."

"That's possible. I now believe the crystal came from the Ancient Ones, perhaps one of the reasons you need to see them. It may be a gift to aid you in your quest."

"Well, if that's so, I can hardly wait to meet them and clear this up. Will you keep it for me? I'm afraid I'd be too tempted to read everyone's thoughts. It's unnerving, and I don't want to make enemies of them."

"No, Angel. I can't."

"Why not?"

He showed her the hand that had held it. Blisters formed as they watched. "It burned me when you tried to read my thoughts. I think only you can touch it. Perhaps this is why you were told to keep it secret."

"If that's so, why didn't it burn your mother?"

"Perhaps it did. I can't answer you. I'm sorry, Angel. This is one burden you have to carry on your own. I wish I could help."

"I know. I just felt your sorrow." She averted her eyes. "Sorry about that." She felt bad about his burn. If she had left it alone, he wouldn't now have a burn on his hand. At least she knew no one could touch it and try to read her thoughts with it.

"Will you do me a favor, Avery? Teach me how to discipline my mind like you do yours."

"That isn't as easy as I let you believe. We come by it naturally as we grow. The only advice I can give you is to keep your ability secret. No telling how the dwarves would react if they found out you had this ability. The elves in the squad would understand, being used to living among such talent." He paused. "Can you read my thoughts now?"

She looked at him a moment and smiled. "Not at present, no."

"Good. You need not worry what you hear from me. It's not much help, and I may let my guard down at times. I'll talk to the other elves and tell them to do the same. Since I'm the next in line to the throne, they'll do as I ask with no questions."

"Thank you, Avery."

They rose and ambled back to camp. Avery was careful not to touch her. She kept her eyes glued to the ground and nearly ran into Serylda.

"Hey, girl. Careful!" Serylda exclaimed. She put her hand out to steady Angel who shied away. "What's wrong?"

"I'm sorry, Serylda. Nothing's wrong. Excuse me." Angel retreated into the tent.

Great. Now, she'd upset her good friend. Maybe she should tell her? No. Avery had warned her not to share the secret. Still, she needed to tell Serylda something. She left the tent and found Serylda standing outside, a puzzled and hurt look on her face. Serylda's confusion invaded Angel's mind. Not averting eye contact, she steeled herself, trying to control the emotions coming from the dwarf.

"I'm sorry. That was a little abrupt. I wish I could tell you what's wrong with me. But, I can't—not yet. When the time comes that I can tell you, I will. Trust me, please, with the friendship we've developed. I don't want you to feel hurt or anger against me."

Angel felt her friend's emotions ease as anger and hurt were replaced with acceptance. *This could become too easy*, Angel thought.

"I can't stay mad at you. You happen to be the Alastrine Savior. You are the guardian of information you can't reveal, and I have to accept that. Besides, you are also my best friend. So I will trust you."

"Well"—Angel grinned—"I promise I will tell you when I can."

"Be careful. A promise to a dwarf is very serious and binding." Serylda gestured toward the fire. "Let's get something to eat. Smells like Telek has supper ready, even though he hasn't rung the 'dinner bell' yet." The girls laughed and ambled toward the campfire and the gathering squad members.

After supper, those not on watch retired. Angel and Serylda followed Niedra to their tent. Serylda entered while Angel and the cat sat outside the tent entrance. Angel wasn't sleepy. Her thoughts turned to her sister. Alison had been lost to her now for over forty days. With that thought, she went inside and fell asleep.

It seemed no sooner had Angel laid her head down when something woke her. She felt disoriented. Hearing Niedra growl, she both realized and felt the danger nearby.

She looked around the tent. Serylda was on guard duty. The cat stood outside near the entrance. Leaving the tent, Angel walked over to Avery, the cat on her heels.

"Is something wrong?" Avery asked. "Can't you sleep? You have another hour before your watch."

"Both Niedra and I feel danger nearby."

At that moment, Marlon screeched. Cornellius awoke. His concern for his bird invaded Angel's mind. He rose and joined them near the fire, the falcon chattering on his arm.

"Marlon's acting very strangely. Something isn't right."

Fears were realized when suddenly they found themselves surrounded. Merwyn, Telek, and Serylda were roughly shoved into the firelight, having been taken hostage while on guard duty. Marlon leapt into the air and disappeared at the same time.

Someone pushed through.

Angel gasped.

"Hello, sis," Alison said, walking out from behind the three captives. "Surprise!" She sneered at Angel.

Suddenly, Angel saw an evil essence emanating from her sister. She tried to ignore it. "Thank goodness! I thought you were dead, Alison."

Alison laughed. "Hardly, sis." She made a swooping gesture with her right arm. "I have complete control of this army." She jabbed a finger at Angel. "And it looks like I have complete control of your little group too."

"I don't understand." Angel frowned. She sensed her mind start to shut down, no longer hearing thoughts around her. "What's happened to you?"

"Ahriman showed me the power he'd give me if I joined him. I couldn't refuse his offer. So I joined him, and I've not regretted it. Not even once." She leaned closer to Angel. "I'm sorry, sis, but he owns me. And, anyway, I love him." She backed off and her attention turned to Attor, to the northwest. "I control his army. He loves me that much." She turned back and touched Angel's arm. "Please forgive me."

Angel sensed remorse in that touch, the evil essence dimmed just for an instant. But then Alison pushed her back with the rest of the squad.

"I know what you plan to do. I cannot allow you to destroy Ahriman," said Alison. "For that matter, sis, I can't kill you either. You were my sister."

"I still am, Alison," Angel said softly.

Suddenly Alison lashed out in a violent rage, and Angel found herself on the ground nursing a bloody lip.

"I never want to hear that name again!" Alison shouted. Her eyes turned to stone, and, in a deadly calm voice, she said, "From this time on, my name is and will always be Stormy. Don't ever forget that."

Serylda helped Angel to her feet. Serylda's rage came through to Angel faintly with her touch. *What has happened to my gift? I need to suppress my negative emotions. That must be it.*

"How can you love Ahriman? We were told he's evil. Remember?"

"Can you really say that even though you've never met the man? I know better. These puny beings you call friends are filling your head with lies. Their words mean nothing."

Suddenly, Angel watched the evil essence surrounding Stormy grow as she grabbed Evrak. A knife appeared in her hand and she slit the dwarf's throat in one swift move.

And that's when Angel's mind shut down completely. She heard what went on around her, but didn't comprehend it. It was May 25, their eighteenth birthday, and Alison had killed in cold blood. And she was Stormy now.

"Morgh, put my prisoners in that cave we found back there. And seal the entrance once you do that." Stormy grabbed one of her men and pulled him close. She laid the still bloody knife blade against his throat. "Don't hurt them any more than necessary, Morgh. And don't kill any one of them or I'll kill you. Understand?"

"Yes, my queen." Morgh bowed low.

She let him go, taking a length of rope from him. "I'm serious. If just one dies, you die. I will know if you disobey. So, you'd better keep a tight rein on your men. I want our prisoners to die by suffocation, slowly."

He nodded and ordered his men to round up the members of the squad toward a pile of boulders near an overhang. Angel's hands were bound in front of her as tears streamed down her face. Stormy made sure the knots were tight. Angel didn't struggle but stared at Avery as he and the others were led to the cave. He opened his mind and sent her a strong feeling of love and assurance before she was led away in the opposite direction.

Angel remembered nothing after that. Stormy kept her hand on the rope binding and pulled her roughly along. Morgh returned to report that he and his men had shoved the prisoners into the cave and sealed the entrance. Only then did Stormy and her army head north into the Rocky Mountains, accompanied by an unresponsive Angel.

———————————

It sounded as if the entire mountain had crashed on top of them. Someone screamed in pain. A few moments later, all was quiet and pitch black. Someone moaned while another rummaged through a pack. When Stormy's men grabbed them, the squad members had managed to maintain possession of their packs, and, luckily, Stormy's men hadn't been smart enough to confiscate them. Telek's face shone for an instant when he struck steel to flint.

"Again."

Barak's voice came out of the darkness. Telek struck his flint over and over until several of the other men hastily fashioned a torch using dry materials they found on the floor of the cave. They had to make and light two more torches before there was enough light to see by.

"Now," Barak began, "let's see how badly off we are." He checked the blocked entrance. "Air is leaving the cave here. See? The smoke from our torches is escaping! We need to find where it's coming in, and try to get out from there. If we can't, we will concentrate on unblocking this entrance. We cannot give up escaping this tomb."

"Barak," Serylda spoke up. "I think you need to come here." Fynbar lay on the floor near the back of the cave. Serylda stood over him. "He's badly hurt. I think a part of the ceiling fell on him."

Barak checked their dear friend. He motioned Avery to him. Fynbar was bleeding from several places, and more bones were broke than not.

"Will he die?" Serylda's voice quivered.

"I'm afraid so," Avery said quietly. "I'm sorry."

She looked down at the dwarf. He smiled at her and whispered the words, "It will be okay. Don't mourn me. Get out and rescue Angel."

"There's nothing to be done," Barak stated. He stood. "We still need to find a way out or we will all die."

They moved Fynbar to the center of the cave and made him as comfortable as possible. Serylda stayed with the dwarf. The others probed the walls in search of drafts. If they could discover where the air entered the room, perhaps they could devise a way to exit their tomb as Barak had planned. After all, they made their living working with stone. Their packs at hand, they still had all their tools.

"Barak!" Serylda's voice held a touch of panic. She stood and motioned him over. "Fynbar wants you."

A tear slid down her face when Fynbar moaned. She sat back down beside him and took his hand in hers. "I'm here. Barak's coming. We won't leave you alone." She felt a slight pressure from his grasp.

Barak squatted beside them. "I'm here, dear friend."

"Promise me you won't let them win. Get out of here and find her. Defeat Ahriman for all those he's wronged." His voice fell silent as he took one last breath and died.

Serylda looked deeply into her brother's eyes. Tears streamed down her face freely. He squeezed her shoulder.

"Come," he whispered. "It's over." He bent down and helped her to her feet. "Let's get out of here. We don't have time to mourn. We have a job to do. I blame Ahriman. He has a lot to answer for besides this one death."

They joined the others and resumed their search for a way out of their tomb. Half an hour later, they gave up. No one could find the small draft entering their room from somewhere in the back of the cave. Barak went over to the blocked entrance and could no longer feel the air escaping.

The dwarves stuck the torches into the center of the dirt floor. They laid Fynbar to rest in the center of the cave and piled rocks over his body. Afterward, no one spoke. Each kept to his or her thoughts. Despair ran rampant. Two hours went by. Then, three. Still no one broke the silence.

"Well," Barak began as he rose. "We need to start on that entrance. We've mourned long enough."

Avery rose and walked over to the rear of the cave. "Listen!" he said.

Barak joined him. "Something's scratching on the wall."

"Yes," Avery agreed. "I think I know who, or should I say, what. It's Niedra. I sense her. She's trying to help us."

Barak looked skeptical. "I can't believe a badgercat would help us. It's not in their nature. Are you sure that's what you sense?"

They heard the cat growl. It was Niedra. Everyone recognized it. Avery found a crack they had all missed earlier. They listened as the cat clawed its way toward them. Everyone grabbed tools and began digging. An hour later, they had dug themselves free through the back of the cave and into a small passageway. The elves resealed the room. It was now, and would be forevermore, the Tomb of Mourning and a lasting monument to all who would perish in the coming storm.

It took nearly three hours to reach the outside. Niedra led the way. They stopped several times to enlarge the passage enough for them to crawl through. They had been entombed nearly a full day.

Outside at last, Avery turned to Barak. "It's your call."

"Can we catch them?"

"We may not be able to, but I think the cat can."

"Then tell it to find Angel, and we'll follow it."

Avery nodded. He bent down and placed a hand on the animal's huge head. "Find Angel," he said aloud.

The cat gave a loud screech and leapt away. It was out of sight and hearing in a matter of moments, an easy feat in the darkening environment.

"That's not quite what I meant, Avery."

"Me, either, friend."

Barak looked at each member of the squad before turning his gaze to the north. "Well, the best we can do is follow."

Everyone agreed. Barak led the way as once more they were on the move. This time they followed the huge cat's prints and traveled farther into the shadowy Rocky Mountains.

"I hope Angel's okay," Serylda said to no one in particular.

"She is," Avery reassured her and the others. "Somehow I feel her spirit."

—◦◦◦◦◦◦—

Angel's days were filled with misery. The way grew steep, yet Stormy kept her army traveling at a fast pace. Consequently, Angel fell several times, only to be jerked upright by Stormy. And the march north continued. At night, they tied her to a tree and gave her food and water while a guard stood watch over her.

She ate and drank nothing for three days. Stormy expressed concern that she might die, and ordered her men to force liquids down her throat. May ended and June arrived before Angel came back to the present. They were on the move when Angel took stock of her surroundings.

The mountains in the near distance appeared rugged and steep. Boulders lay strewn across their path. And the trees stood so numerous, they blocked the mountains from sight most of the time. She recognized the Rockies; they looked the same to her as they had in her previous life.

Her arms and legs hurt from the bruises she had suffered. She had fallen so many times she felt like a punching bag. The way some of her injuries felt, she was grateful she didn't remember receiving them.

That evening Stormy ordered her men to set up camp as she tied Angel to a tree, as usual.

"Well, sis. Did you finally decide to join us?" She stood in front of Angel, her hands resting on her hips, her feet spread wide.

Angel said nothing. She just stared off in the distance.

"Okay, don't talk. I don't care. I just want you to know we'll be arriving at Attor in about three weeks. It would've been sooner but ..." She sat down next to Angel as she had when they were young. "We're traveling straight through. And that means marching through these dratted mountains." She smiled and placed a hand on Angel's right arm. "Join us, sis. You wouldn't regret it. Trust me. We three—Ahriman, you, and I—could rule the world. Think about that. It'd be wondrous."

"No," Angel said softly. The evil essence still surrounded her sister.

"I bet Ahriman can change your mind when you see him. How about it? Wanna bet?"

Again Angel said, "No."

"Well, I'm glad you're back with us, at least." Stormy rose. "It'll be nice to get home."

"How long have I been your captive?"

"Oh, eleven days."

"And have we been traveling the whole time?"

"Pretty much so, yes. Why do you ask?"

"Curiosity." Angel closed her eyes and leaned back against the tree. "Just curiosity." Stormy grunted and left.

Eleven days! That would make it around the fourth of June. A long time to be apart from friends. Where was Avery? She couldn't live if he was dead. With that thought swimming in her mind, she cried herself to sleep.

Later that night, Angel was awakened by a presence she hadn't felt in quite some time.

Niedra?

Yes. One gone. The badgercat sent her an image of Fynbar. *Rest, okay?*

She felt sadness for the loss of the dwarf, yet no tears fell. *Where are the others, Niedra?*

Coming. I help. Black one don't think me good. An image of Barak invaded her thoughts.

She smiled. *I'm not surprised. He will come to trust you, Niedra.*

They are here.

Angel looked around discreetly. She spied Avery in the bush to the right of her position. He nodded and sent her feelings of love and relief.

Can you hear me, Angel?

Yes.

Don't be alarmed, but Barak is behind you. The rest are hiding several miles back. We're going to try to release you without warning Ahriman's men. We don't want a fight right now.

Understood. She felt Barak's presence behind her.

She sensed Avery hesitate inside her head. *What's wrong, Avery?*

He paused before answering her. *I don't want you to be alarmed. Niedra's our distraction.*

What? Angel's heart skipped a beat. *Will she be okay?*

Me okay. Got friend help. Niedra sent her an image of another cat nearby. Angel didn't know how to react hearing Niedra "talk" and having two badgercats help them.

Both cats screeched and sent the camp into a frenzy. Angel watched as men jumped up grabbing their weapons. Stormy and her entire army moved toward the sounds as one. Even Angel's guard left to help. The cats stayed in the brush, screeching and moving away from the fires. Now and then she caught sight of orange fur before they were too far away. Niedra reassured Angel she was staying clear of the deadly arrows. *Smart animals*, Angel thought.

Just as she decided the army was far enough away to try to escape, Barak rushed out from his hiding place and cut her bonds. Seconds later they were safely hidden and traveling farther from danger. The plan had worked—so far.

The moon had set for the night. It was pitch black. Several times Angel stubbed her toes and went down. And each time, Barak helped her back to her feet. She needed to be a little more careful. Her body already harbored enough bruises to last her the rest of her life.

Suddenly, Barak grabbed her arm and jerked her hard to him, keeping her from falling into a deep hole. Barak had saved her life! Thank goodness for the keen eyes of dwarves!

Don't be so dramatic, Angel, she admonished herself. *He only kept you from breaking your ankle.*

By dawn, they had rejoined the rest of the squad. Niedra was back too. Serylda gave her a big hug when she saw Angel. Merwyn, his left thigh bandaged, and Derwyn, uninjured, just smiled. Kendrik, a gash on his right forearm, nodded, while Cornellius just stood quietly nearby, looking lost.

Marlon numbered among the missing. Included with the falcon were Javas and Telek. Serylda informed her of the loss of Fynbar.

"Our path lies southwest of here," Barak said. "Telek and Javas know where we are headed. Either they will catch up with us or meet us there, if they still live." He placed a hand on Cornellius's shoulder. "Marlon will have to find us as best he can. All of us here have high hope for his return, my friend."

"I believe if he is alive, he will find me." Cornellius tried to look hopeful and moved away from Barak.

As Cornellius walked past Angel, she placed a hand temporarily over his. She felt his pain and loss. Cornellius truly believed Marlon was gone. She stepped back, and the squad resumed their trek to the

Great Crack. Cornellius's thoughts stayed with Angel, but weren't as strong. She realized she was able to hear thoughts again. The ability had returned as soon as she'd seen Avery in the enemy camp.

Angel had one thing on her mind as they traveled. *Am I fine now?* She seemed to be reading thoughts more easily than before. But it didn't seem to bother her as much. *Am I getting used to alien thoughts invading my own?* She desperately needed to talk to the Ancient Ones. And the sooner, the better.

CHAPTER 10

The Great Crack

I T FELT GOOD TO BE in the desert and out of the mountains. The comradeship among the travelers had grown stronger. Everyone got along better despite the heat and dry air. And they hadn't met any more of Ahriman's men since leaving the Rockies.

Angel learned a few things along the way. Niedra had learned how to "talk" to her with words. It was a gift the badgercat hadn't lost from its native world. Also, she felt her sister was somehow being manipulated by Ahriman. That was the only explanation Angel came up with for the aura of evil that surrounded her sister. That was the only reason she could give for Stormy taking a life. Any belief otherwise made Angel sick.

"How much longer do you think we have to travel before we reach the Great Crack?" Angel asked.

"My guess," Barak answered, "is we'll arrive either tomorrow or the next day."

"We elves agree," Merwyn added.

Angel thought about the date and came up with July thirteenth. The desert wasn't as hot as she thought it should have been.

Avery moved alongside her. "It has been warmer."

"Yes, I wondered about that," Angel said, glancing at Avery, her eyebrows up. He had read her emotions and grinned back.

"Last year," Kendrik broke in, "it was decidedly hotter. I wonder why it's cooler this year."

"Maybe Ahriman has something to do with it," Serylda suggested.

Barak shrugged. "Perhaps. Whatever the reason, I think this is as good a place as any for camp."

They had set up every campsite the same since they left the mountains. Members of the squad erected the girls' tent and gathered firewood. Niedra became their guard, since she sensed anyone near before they came in sight. Kendrik took over the cooking duties while Cornellius still hunted, though without his trusty bird. The gashes Merwyn and Kendrik had experienced were healed. Derwyn helped Kendrik with his duties. Javas and Telek still numbered as missing.

As before, Serylda trained Angel in the art of quarterstaff fighting. The men oiled their weapons while the girls practiced, staying in sight of camp.

That night, Serylda took hold of Angel's arm. "Before we retire, I have a gift."

Angel frowned. "I didn't do anything to deserve a gift."

Serylda grinned. "You've graduated. I can teach you no more. You are ready to fight with the quarterstaff." She entered the tent only to return with a new weapon. "I made this last night while you slept."

Angel hadn't paid attention to it, seeing it in the tent earlier and thinking it was Serylda's. But now she looked closer and realized it was a new one, not the one Serylda used. And it was beautiful. A thought entered her mind. Why hadn't she sensed Serylda's secret? She dismissed it as fast as she had thought it.

When Angel stood the butt end on the ground, the weapon reached six inches above her head. Colorful feathers adorned it. The pointed end stood out from the feathers. At about shoulder high, a piece of leather dyed a rich indigo blue wrapped around the staff.

"Why is it so beautiful if it's a fighting weapon? It seems too ornamental to me. I'd hate to use it in a fight."

"Believe me, it's just as deadly as mine." Serylda sat down and leaned against a tree. "I found the feathers along our trek. When I had enough, I tied them around your staff. All new warriors receive one when they achieve fighting readiness. Mine was just as beautiful when it was new."

"Where did the blue leather come from?" Angel sat beside her friend.

"Telek gave it to me the night before Stormy captured us. He said to give it to you when you become proficient enough to earn this weapon. At that time, he knew you were almost ready."

"Thank you, Serylda. I will always remember what you have done for me. And I am honored that Telek felt so sure of me."

Serylda picked up a nearby stick and toyed with it. "There remains one thing left to do. You must fight Barak." She glanced at Angel before returning her attention back to the stick in her hand. "Show some restraint. Don't humiliate him too much. But do show him you have complete control of this weapon."

Angel grinned. "In other words, give him a bloody nose and not regret it."

"Well, kind of, yes." Serylda frowned. "I did imagine you doing that." She threw her stick away, leaned back, and closed her eyes.

Oops! Angel had better keep a tighter rein on her mouth. She rose and went in search of Barak. *Better get this trial over,* she thought. She found him sitting by the fire with the other members of the squad. Niedra, lying near the tent entrance, kept alert of her surroundings, even with her eyes closed.

Everything clear? she asked the cat.

Yes. Niedra stretched and yawned.

Don't worry about what's fixing to happen. Barak and I are going to pretend fight to test my ability to use this weapon.

Okay. The cat rose and padded to the rear of the tent. *I stay back here so Black One stay calm.*

Angel smiled and walked to the fire. The cat simply refused to use Barak's name. Still, Angel felt lucky to have such an animal as protector and companion … a companion only she could mind read.

"Barak, I'm ready for your test." She held up the new quarterstaff.

Rising, Barak yelled at his sister. "Bring me your staff." Serylda did so and handed him her weapon. An area near the fire was made ready, and the test began.

The clacking of the weapons slamming together reverberated throughout the camp. With cheers from the onlookers, the test continued for five long minutes. Angel kept a tight rein on her mind, truly wanting to prove to herself she had control of the quarterstaff. Then, suddenly …

Angel tripped on her own feet. Losing control, she allowed herself to "hear" Barak's thoughts. Knowing he would step left, she anticipated his move. Using one end of her new weapon, she tripped him and twirled the quarterstaff around. Using the other end, she knocked his weapon out of his hands and jabbed him in the face.

Nose bloodied, Barak found himself on the ground unarmed. Angel stood over him triumphant and smiling, her feet spread wide and her weapon still in hand. The butt end rested on the ground in front of her.

"Well?" she asked even though she knew what his response would be.

"Serylda taught you well." He rose and retrieved Serylda's staff from where it had fallen a few feet away and returned it to its owner. He bent down and plucked a certain weed. Using it, he staunched his bloody nose and turned back to Angel. "You've passed, as I'm sure you know. Congratulations."

"Thank you." She bowed and turned. Everyone watched her. She sensed their satisfaction in her performance, especially Kendrik's. He felt impressed with the speed with which she had disarmed his leader.

Still, she felt she had cheated. She harbored an advantage no one but Avery knew about. She knew what Barak had planned to do before he did it. It was unintentional, though. This was one of those times she wished she could turn off her newfound talent. It would have made the test more accurate in revealing her ability. And she felt guilty for bloodying Barak's nose.

"Supper's ready," Kendrik called.

After supper everyone gathered around the fire. Barak nodded at Avery. Obviously the elf had something to say. "Before we retire, I have some information everyone needs to hear." Avery looked at each in turn to make sure all were listening. "Barak and I have studied our maps. We believe we'll arrive at the Great Crack sometime tomorrow evening."

"Barring nothing happens like meeting more of Ahriman's men," Kendrik added.

"Exactly, my friend," Barak agreed.

"When we arrive," Avery continued, "Angel and I will hunt out the Ancient Ones' cave. Once that is done, Angel will go in alone."

"Alone?" Angel squeaked. "I have to go in alone? I was hoping you'd go with me."

"I'm sorry, no. Only you will seek them out, Angel," Avery answered. "They won't appear to anyone else."

"Our Legend says only the Alastrine Savior can see them," Merwyn spoke up.

"So," Barak interrupted, "let's retire for the night and dream of finishing this journey tomorrow."

Angel stayed where she was and watched as everyone else called it a day. They were all in agreement. She felt their confidence about finding the Ancient Ones and defeating Ahriman. She wished she had as much confidence in herself as they had for her.

Angel rose and went inside the tent. Niedra kept her vigil outside the entrance as she had done since Angel's rescue from Stormy. She proved to be a better guard than any person in the squad. Serylda was snoring, deep into whatever dreams played in her head. Angel vaguely realized she didn't hear the dreams. Her mind was on her own dilemma as she slipped into her sleeping bag.

Her heart pounded at the prospect of going into the cave alone. Not because it was a cave. But because she was doing it to meet creatures who were supposed to tell her how to defeat a powerful, immortal being that no one else had ever been able to beat. *Why me? Can I actually do it? How?* She fell asleep with those thoughts roaming in her mind unanswered.

The squad set off early the next morning. Breakfast had been a rushed affair. All were eager to finish their trek. Their thoughts had become so familiar to her. She hardly noticed them inside her mind now. When had that happened?

Niedra scouted ahead for danger. No one seemed worried about coming into contact with Ahriman's men. They felt they had gone far enough south. Consequently, they didn't try to be quiet. The travelers maintained conversations at a loud timbre the entire day.

The day turned out to be very hot, one of the warmest of their journey. Angel's hat kept the sun off her face, but did little to relieve the heat. In just a few hours she had become sticky and dirty, which made her day long and tiring.

Just before sunset, the squad arrived at the Great Crack. They set up camp several hundred yards away from the rim of the canyon. It was too dark to get any closer, let alone go below the rim. That could wait for dawn.

Angel sensed the great chasm but couldn't see where the rim began. It would be a very dark night. The moon was absent, being a new one. She felt the emptiness, the vastness, of the great hole in the ground, and kept well away from it.

After supper, the girls retired to their tent. The men stayed by the fire and enjoyed its warmth a little longer.

"Are you ready for tomorrow? I'm excited for you." Serylda climbed into her sleeping bag.

"No," Angel answered, getting into bed too. "I'm afraid of heights. I thought I could do this. I really don't know if I can. I'm not ready." She drew in a deep breath before letting it out slowly.

"Well, my friend, you need to figure out how to get over that. You have to go down. No one else will be able to do it for you. It is, after all, your destiny."

"I know." Angel lay down. "I'll just have to find the courage. I guess we'd better get some sleep." Though she doubted she'd be able to sleep a wink.

Angel remained awake as she had feared. She'd heard the men retire at least an hour ago. All she could think about was that giant crack in the ground a few hundred yards from her. She had never visited the Grand Canyon in her youth. She'd only seen pictures of it. Even back then, it had given her feelings of dread. The feelings were stronger now. *Will I panic tomorrow? And if I do, will I be able to control my fear?* The members of the squad, as one, were excited. Their legend was coming to life. Their oppression from Ahriman was nearing an end. They had arrived at their destination, and the Alastrine Savior was going to meet the Ancient Ones. No panic, only excitement.

Oh, why was I chosen for this task? Why couldn't it have been Alison? She's the more daring one.

Angel bolted upright. She hadn't thought of her twin for quite some time now. She was somewhat ashamed of herself. She wondered what Alison was doing right now. *Does she still live?* Oh, if she hadn't listened to Alison that fateful day, they wouldn't be here now. Angel hadn't wanted to stray from the trail. Not really. It had been her twin's idea. Alison's adventurous side always got them into trouble. And visiting the caverns had been her sister's idea too.

Stop, Angel, she chided herself. She had to be honest with herself. She had enjoyed going to Carlsbad Caverns. She just hadn't wanted to veer off the designated trail. Yet, she had allowed Alison … no, Stormy … to talk her into it. Well, both girls were in a pickle now.

Darkness still covered the land when she heard the men stirring outside. She hadn't slept a wink. Her heart pounded when she rose and left the warmth of the tent. The flap faced away from the canyon. At least her first sight wouldn't be of it.

The fire beckoned with warmth, roaring with fresh wood. She joined the men at the fire, being careful to not look backward.

"Good morning," Avery greeted. "Are you ready for our trek this morning?"

"No." Angel sat, dread showing in her face. "I have something to confess. I'm deathly afraid of heights. I was hoping my fear would be gone by the time we reached here. But it's still there. I'm sorry." She cupped her face in her hands.

"Great!" Barak huffed and slapped his thigh. "How is Angel supposed to find the Ancient Ones if she can't climb down to do so?"

Avery smiled reassuringly at Angel. "Don't worry. She will find the courage. And I will be with her to the cave entrance."

Angel felt his thoughts bump her own. She realized how easy it had become to read others, except the elves. They had done a fine job helping her, though she knew not how. Avery sent her feelings of deep love and assurance, just like the feelings he'd sent when she had been Stormy's captive.

Trust me, he thought to her.

She had a question. *Avery, can you read my thoughts?*

Only the ones you allow. I cannot read thoughts like you can.

Thank you. I love you, too, Avery. I will trust my life to you. She allowed him to feel the deep trust she had in him.

"Be reassured, Barak. Everything will be fine." Avery's smile deepened. "We shall make our descent after breakfast." He rose and began gathering the things he thought they'd need.

Serylda exited the tent. "Well, how's everything? Where's breakfast?"

"Angel is afraid of heights," Kendrik informed her and handed her a bowl of cooked beans.

"I know. She told me last night." Serylda huddled near the fire and dug into the beans. "I have faith in her, Kendrik. Shouldn't you too?"

"Well, we shall see, won't we?" he answered back.

Angel listened in on their conversation and their thoughts. Even though Kendrik voiced misgivings, he had the same faith in her as did the rest of the squad. *I just wish I knew what I'm supposed to do,* she pondered. *What if I don't defeat Ahriman? What happens then? What will he do?*

Ten minutes passed. Avery helped Angel to her feet. She turned toward the canyon. She took a deep breath and let it out fast. It was time for her to face her fear.

The Grand Canyon wasn't like the pictures she remembered as a child. It was worse! Her eyes measured the distance from the edge of the drop-off to the other side of the canyon. She felt the nothingness that filled the giant gap.

The awesome emptiness gnawed her insides, and the depth turned her knees to jelly. As she crept closer to the edge, her fear of heights rose with a vengeance. Her knees gave out, and she went down on all fours. She crawled to the edge and looked down. Her first sight filled her with relief. The bottom of the canyon lay enshrouded in fog. At least her first real look into the depths muted the reality of the depth that so frightened her.

Still on hands and knees, she glanced back toward camp. Everyone stared. Their disappointment was strong in her mind. She must really look silly.

Avery stood nearby. He smiled and held out his hand. Very gingerly, she took hold of it and rose with his help.

"I'm terrified," she confessed in a whisper. She didn't want the others to hear her words. She had disappointed them enough.

"I know." He held her hand tightly, reassuringly. "I won't let you go."

She nodded as he pulled her close. She allowed him to lead her down into the Great Crack.

Below the lip, Angel made out a faint animal trail that disappeared into the fog. She kept her mind active by thinking of the trails that used to be here, perhaps filled with people braver than she. As they descended, using the faint trail for guidance, she felt the utter vastness of the canyon. She was glad for the fog, as the emptiness didn't abate.

No, she wasn't being truthful to herself. She wasn't glad. She was terrified and hoped the fog lasted forever. Only her hand in Avery's gave her the courage to put one foot in front of the other. *And they want me to defeat Ahriman? I can't even get down into this canyon without help!*

Halfway down, panic set in. The fog lifted. Angel thought they were near bottom. But what she saw nearly made her faint. Mother Earth had opened up and swallowed her. She wasn't coming out alive.

Why do people enjoy coming here? This was worse than anything Angel had ever experienced in her young life. This vast hole made her feel so small and lost. Mother Earth kept asking her why she attempted to enter her domain. She closed her eyes and her body trembled.

"Easy, Angel." Avery squeezed her hand. "I'm here. You won't fall."

She opened her eyes. She had forgotten he was so near. *Why?* "I wish I didn't have such a fear of heights, Avery." She tried to laugh, but it turned into a near cry of terror.

"Trust me," he reassured her as he led her farther into the depths. "I will not let go of your hand."

"I know. I'm being silly. I realize that. But sometimes when emotions take over, we lose control. Besides, my problem is a kind of disease where I come from. It even has a name."

"Tell me," Avery said. She sensed that he realized talking helped her calm her nerves.

"It's called acrophobia. It's an irrational fear of heights. And I have it bad."

"A peculiar word." He helped her past an unusually large boulder.

Angel smiled, her fear eased a little. "I thought so, too, the first time I heard it."

"We should be getting close to the entrance."

"It's not at the bottom?"

"No, Angel. The bottom is still a long way down. I've been here only once and was too young to remember the way. According to our legend, an animal track leads directly to the entrance. We have to follow each faint trail we come across until we find the right one."

"Great." Angel shuddered. "And, I assume they are all at this height?"

"Pretty much so, yes."

Once more they worked their way past another giant boulder. The trail wound through a crack between boulder and canyon wall. It proved too small for them to fit through, forcing them to find a way around. On the other side the trail disappeared.

"Our first dead end," Avery said. "Time to start back up. We can make it back to camp a little after lunch." They turned around and retraced their course.

"I was so hoping this was it. Especially after what you said earlier." Angel kept a tight hold on Avery's proffered hand. "I'm not looking forward to doing this again."

"You will survive, Angel. We all believe in you. Believe in yourself. Trust your instincts."

"I'm trying. Only your help has gotten me this far."

"I know. I've felt your terror." He stopped in a fairly wide part of the path, took both of her hands in his, and looked deeply into her eyes. "Use your mind to gain strength from mine. Feel my courage and use it to boost your own."

"How in the world am I supposed to do that?"

"I can't tell you how. Each person has that ability but needs to learn it through experience. Our children sometimes need their parents' strength, and they do this thing naturally. You will just have to try."

She took a deep breath and concentrated on him, still trying to shy away from his thoughts. She felt the deep self-confidence he allowed her to experience. Concentrating on it, she used it to boost her own. It seemed to help a little. She felt it might be enough to get her back to camp as he led the way up. She thanked him when she caught a glimpse of the campfire. She had made it in one piece.

A surprise greeted them upon their arrival. Telek had found them. After recounting his adventures to the two, he excused himself. He harbored a half-healed broken left arm and was tired.

"How was it?" Serylda asked as soon as Telek left.

"Terrifying." Angel sat down near the fire trying to get warm. Although it was just past noon and becoming hotter, she sat shivering. "I have to go back, Serylda. We didn't find the entrance to the cave. We plan on going the other way after we eat."

"Here you go." Kendrik handed her a bowl of stew. Serylda sat quietly as Angel ate.

An hour passed before Angel and Avery were on a trail he had found a mile east of camp. Instead of eating, he had been hunting another way down. The sun had burned off the fog, and Angel saw the canyon in all its grandeur.

Although Angel was still terrified, her fear didn't seem as bad. Avery held her hand as before, and she gained strength from it. Even with his help, she harbored a feeling of utter awe at the sight facing her. With Avery's help, she controlled her fear more easily than she previously had. Traversing boulders proved easier as well.

Then, an unusually large boulder blocked their path. Avery couldn't see any way around it. Shrubbery hugged the canyon and made it impossible to sidestep the boulder. When Angel disturbed a branch, she spied a crack in the wall and moved more vegetation out of the way. They uncovered a crack in the wall large enough to allow a normal-sized adult to enter.

"That's it," Avery announced. "That's the entrance to the Ancient Ones' cave. I feel it."

"Funny," Angel spoke up. "I can feel that too. I wonder why?"

"Your crystal." He let go of her hand. "Is it warm?"

She felt of the crystal. "Yes, it is. I can tell it is trying to guide me somehow. It says this is it." She closed her eyes and stepped back a little, tripped on a rock and nearly fell off the cliff. Her heart beat with fear.

"Careful, Angel." Avery grabbed her. "Now that we're here, I'd hate to lose you from a fall. It would be a great tragedy, to be sure."

She grabbed his hand in a tight grip. "Come with me," she pleaded.

"You know I can't, Angel." He shook his head. "This is your quest. Not mine." Gently he pulled his hands out of hers.

"But, it's so dark in there." She pointed to the crack. "I can't see. I'm not like the dwarves."

"Check your crystal, Angel. I believe you'll find it is glowing."

She pulled it from her tunic, and, indeed, it was glowing. Something called to her. She couldn't disobey. Forgetting Avery, she entered the cave. Strange, she felt at home. She didn't know why, but didn't argue with herself.

Once completely inside, she realized all mental contact with Avery had ceased. She no longer felt or heard his thoughts. Even the faint signature of the squad's thoughts had ceased. She didn't worry about it but continued deeper into the cave.

The tunnel she found herself in seemed endless. Deeper and deeper her feet carried her. Where were the Ancient Ones? She felt they were close. But her crystal showed more tunnel ahead.

She kept walking until she finally reached the end. A gigantic boulder stood in her way. She contemplated what to do. She needed to be on the other side. Somehow she knew this. As she watched, the boulder began to move, and a passage opened up beyond. Slowly she entered this new passageway. It proved to be shorter than the previous one. It led to a room one-fourth the size of the Big Room in Jasper. An arch became visible on the opposite wall. She moved toward it. It led to one more room, smaller than the first. Inside, she set eyes on the Ancient Ones. All but two stood against the opposite wall.

"Welcome, Angel. We've been expecting you."

CHAPTER 11

S HE HAD MADE IT. THE Ancient Ones were in front of her. She saw the resemblance between Queen Kalika and these beings. The pointed ears and dark hair were the same. They stood six feet or more and wore robes of a pale gauze-type fabric over their willowy frames. Both wore smiles on their faces, putting her at ease immediately.

"Don't be afraid, Angel. We are here to help you," said the one closest to her with a deep voice. *Male perhaps?*

"I think I'm more surprised than frightened." She checked her surroundings. Only two of the Ancient Ones paid any attention to her. Four others stood unmoving against one wall. "Who are you? Where did you come from?"

"We will answer your questions momentarily. First, we will see to your comfort." This one sounded female, her voice higher pitched than the other. They led her to another room behind them. Angel shrugged and followed.

A table flanked by two benches, all carved from rock, stood in the middle of the room. The female left through a small doorway. When she returned carrying a pitcher and three glasses, she placed her burden on the table, and the two Ancient Ones sat on one of the benches. Angel thought it interesting and joined them, sitting on the opposite bench.

"We are glad you survived your trip here. We know of your trials along the way." The male bowed his head. "Your world is now harsher than it was in the time you come from. I'm sorry, you may call me Yondel."

He had read her mind, but Angel felt no anger over it. She had just been on the verge of asking him his name.

"And my name is Zema," said the female. She reached for the pitcher and filled the glasses. She handed the first one to Angel. "This will help you stay alert as we talk. We have much to impart onto you."

"What is this?"

"A fruit drink from our planet. The only thing we've been able to save from our home besides the badgercat, which we are saddened to find has been transformed into a vicious animal."

Angel accepted the glass and sat it down in front of her. "I'll drink some later. I'm not thirsty at present. Thank you."

Zema bowed to her consensus. "It is time to begin." She looked over at Yondel and nodded.

"We are from what your time called Proxima Centauri," Yondel commenced.

"I remember that name from school," Angel said. "It's our nearest star."

"Yes," said Zema. "It is a little over four light years away, in your reckoning."

"We came here to aid you in healing your world." Yondel lowered his head. "We knew what was to come by the looks of your technology. You were in danger of destroying your world. Your pollution was well underway to becoming unrestrained. Your learning and advancement had evolved to a stage that was very dangerous."

"What do you mean?"

"Please do not take it wrong. Compared to our technology, you were babes. Your world was on its way to being highly polluted by a variety of extremely dangerous substances."

"And our scientists proved it true," interrupted Zema. "Your world was dying. Its death may have been a few hundred years into your future, but it was a fact. We could not let that happen. Our world was nearly dead for the same reasons. A few of us were chosen to aid you, while a multitude of others left our planet in search for another world to colonize. We didn't realize our mistake in time, but we were optimistic we could help you save yours."

"My world was dying?"

"Without our help," Yondel continued, "your planet would have been dead in as little as five hundred years. We wanted to divert that disaster."

"But it didn't work the way you planned, right?" Angel took a sip of her drink without realizing it. She just knew her throat was dry.

"You are correct," Yondel said. "In order for you to understand our dilemma, you need to know more about our people."

Zema took up the narration as both Angel and Yondel took sips of their drinks.

"Our planet was a peaceful one. We nearly destroyed ourselves several times. Our negative emotions were rapidly overtaking our minds. Factions arose. More than a hundred were scattered throughout our planet. They decreed that the religious sects were obsolete. They hated the sect that wanted the people to learn control and become peaceful. The religious sect had become so powerful, the factions united to defeat them. The religious sect nearly became extinct."

Yondel continued the tale. "The religious sect had a very good reason to try to control the people. They had accidentally revealed that they owned a powerful secret that could change the world. The factions didn't like not having the secret they thought was the answer to the control of the world.

"That secret turned up in several of our citizens who turned to the religious sect for help. We were learning how to develop what you would call extrasensory perception talents—ESP. Some even learned how to use it to torture and kill. The religious sect could not let that go on. Remember, we said we were a peaceful people."

Zema lowered her head in shame. She allowed Angel to feel some of the emotion so she could better understand the Ancient Ones' disgrace.

"Once the secret came out," Yondel continued, "the factions realized how dangerous this talent could become. They joined the religious sect to inform and teach our people the correct way to use this phenomenon.

"It would become a tremendous task. It was the beginning of our awakening. Before we accomplished the task, our people were nearly destroyed. The people started agreeing to the help when both sects and factions offered the training."

Zema raised her head and said, "As we learned more, we also learned we could control our negative emotions and release them from ourselves."

"How did you do that?" Angel took another sip of her juice.

"Well, with the breakthrough," Zema said, "our scientists learned another thing that taught us about our talent. They were working on our genetic makeup. They found we harbored a gene tied into this talent and another tied into our emotional states. They were connected somehow after mutating from the damage we'd done to our planet. The scientists learned how to eradicate the negative chromosome, and when they did—"

"When they did," Yondel interrupted, "we lost our negative, evil emotions and gained a better bonding with our paranormal talents. Also, it gave our race a longer life span. Our average age went from around one hundred years to over two thousand years."

"I'm lost," Angel said and took another sip. The juice was addictive. "How does all this tie into our world?"

Yondel drank the remaining juice in his cup and poured more for himself. He offered to refill hers. Smiling, Angel shook her head no.

"Remember, we learned we were too late to save our world," Yondel said. "But with our emotions stabilized, our longer life spans, and our paranormal talents, we no longer felt the need to destroy. We became a nonviolent race able to explore. It was our hope to find a new world."

"That is when we noticed your planet," said Zema.

"Ah, now we are getting to why I'm here." She finished her drink. It had been better than she first thought it would be. It tasted different than anything she had ever drunk before. Angel wondered if they had drugged her.

Zema smiled. "Trust me, it was only fruit juice from our planet. And, yes, now we shall address why you are here."

The Centauri looked at each other with shame. They allowed Angel to see and feel their reluctance, which was shadowed with their determination to tell her their problem. Yondel nodded at Zema, who started to explain.

"One of our own has turned evil," she said. "Ahriman is responsible for your planet's destruction and subsequent fall into anarchy." Zema rose and picked up the empty pitcher. "I'll return with food and more juice," she said.

Yondel took up the narration. "Ahriman was the son of our expedition leader. One day, after landing on your planet, he disappeared. We sought out your president for help. Before then, no one on your planet knew we were here. A month passed. Ahriman reappeared with an ultimatum. He was to be given total control of Earth or he'd have his followers destroy it with weapons he'd fashioned from our vessel. He found factions on your world who became loyal to him."

"We couldn't comprehend his actions," Zema said reentering the room. She set a tray filled with fruit and vegetables down on the table along with another pitcher of fruit juice. "His emotional state was foreign to us by then."

"To prove his point," Yondel said, "he destroyed our space vessel. We were stranded on your planet. He warned us to worship him or he'd destroy this world with all its inhabitants. No one could go back to Proxima Centauri for help. With the destruction of our vessel, we lost all contact with our homeworld."

"By now," Zema said, "our people in our homeworld will have assumed there were no survivors. They would have noticed a nuclear war breaking out."

Angel helped herself to a piece of fruit. It tasted like the juice. Very refreshing. "What happened?"

"We disagreed with Ahriman. Remember, we said we couldn't comprehend his actions." Zema took a drink and continued.

"About a week before these events took place, Earth suffered a major theft. To enhance the weapons he made, Ahriman stole several quantities of nuclear waste from different locations throughout your world. How this happened, we aren't sure. It was such a major theft, no country imparted the news to the public. They kept the thefts secret to keep the people from panicking. It happened about thirty years after your time, which is why you never knew of the apocalypse about to be released.

"Our refusal to do as Ahriman had demanded gave him reason to use his weapons. One was detonated aboard our vessel. Another was placed with a terrorist group loyal to Ahriman but against your America, which he thought was the strongest country at the time. Our refusal gave the terrorists good reason to use their bomb on New York City. The United States military panicked, and World War Three began." Again Zema hung her head in shame. "We had lost control of one of our own. We who had come to help you, only helped destroy your world."

Yondel took up the narration once more. "Remember, for one of us to turn so evil was beyond our imagining. We were a peaceful people. So, we kept asking ourselves: Why? What happened to turn Ahriman evil, to revert to those negative emotions we thought had been eradicated? We have yet to figure that out."

"And this is where I come in," Angel stated, realizing this was what they wanted her to do—discover the source of Ahriman's evil.

"Yes," they said in unison.

"You will have to do better than that if you want my help."

"We believe," said Zema, "only one such as yourself, from this planet, who hasn't been influenced by our presence may be able to learn what we cannot. Someone from your time, someone from before our visit was known."

"Okay," Angel said. "There's only one thing wrong with that reasoning. You're suggesting you went into the past. That is impossible."

"We have the ability to move through time," Yondel confessed. "It is one revelation the religious sect kept a tight secret." Yondel bit into a piece of an orange vegetable that reminded Angel of squash.

"We are part of that sect—the ones you see here along the wall and ourselves," Zema said. "We can move through time but at a tremendous cost to ourselves. It steals from our life force, shortening our existence. The bodies along the wall are dead and in stasis. When we who are left have accomplished what we set out to do, we will die, and this cave will collapse, forever sealing us in."

Yondel sighed. "There were eight of us stranded on your planet, including Ahriman. Four offered to sacrifice themselves to bring you and Alison to this time."

"In the Earth year 2025," Zema continued, "four Centauri went back thirty years to Carlsbad Caverns. Two died in the process. The other two, Yondel and I, found your sister and you wandering the caves, lost. We placed you both in a deep sleep to ease the return trip through time and brought you forward the thirty years we had traveled. We realized we had not used all our life force on this colossal task. We believe this was so because Yondel and I were the youngest of the four. Only one other was younger.

"Our leader decided on a different course of action than originally planned. He and Shefor volunteered to transport you two as far into the future as they could go. The remaining three of us stayed and began what is known as the Alastrine Legend to keep the hope alive."

"You see," Yondel interrupted, "though we knew you, we didn't know when you'd reappear. The two volunteers were to use nearly all their life force in their endeavor. They sacrificed themselves to give us time to try to solve our dilemma on our own before relying on you."

"And you lost," Angel stated.

"We lost," they said together.

"Who are those standing against the wall in the other room?"

"Those are the ones who gave their lives to bring you to this time." Yondel sighed. "When they accomplished their tasks, their bodies materialized in this cavern. We hunted for twenty years before we found this cavern, being drawn by our kind. Their spirits still remain, though their bodies are dead. We remain here as guardians, awaiting the end of Ahriman's evil in this world."

Zema looked at Angel. "I believe you've figured out that Queen Kalika was the youngest of us. She became the keeper of the legend and the stone you now carry. We disappeared so we could return to answer your questions once you arrived here."

"In here, we were able to slow our lives down enough to survive to this day when you would need us," said Yondel.

"Kalika became the mother of the Elfin Nation," Zema continued. "The blending of Centauri and human DNA kept both races alive. Kalika, Yondel, and I are the last true Centauri, besides Ahriman."

"That's very interesting, but you still haven't explained why you chose me."

"You possess a gentle spirit, Angel." Yondel paused before continuing. "I'm sorry, but your sister doesn't. She has a wilder nature than yours. Only one such as you would do, we believe. We brought your sister along for your benefit. Both of you awoke to a new and different world, one filled with evil you two had never faced. Everything you knew is a distant memory now."

"Okay, I've pretty much accepted that now. One question: what does having a gentle spirit have to do with it?"

"You are opposite everything Ahriman is now. Only one like you can determine why he is as he is."

"We cannot get near him," Zema said. "He can sense one like himself, a Centauri. We all can sense each other."

"Well, if I'm supposed to defeat him, how am I to accomplish this?" Angel felt herself warming up to these aliens who had so tragically been marooned on her planet.

"You will learn in time," Zema answered.

"Meaning you don't know," Angel retorted. *Great. I came here to get answers but receive riddles.* "Well, changing the subject, I wonder if you can help me on something else. I have acquired the ability to read other people's thoughts and emotions. I can't seem to hear yours, though I have felt you touching my mind. Can you help me?"

"When did this begin?" Zema asked.

"Shortly after we left Krikor, after I received this crystal."

The Centauri looked at each other. "The crystal?" Yondel asked.

"Must be," Zema answered. She turned to Angel. "May I touch you?"

"Why?" Angel asked with apprehension.

"To see the extent of this ability. I will not hurt you."

"I guess," she agreed reluctantly. Her heart pounded.

Zema took hold of Angel's hands and closed her eyes. Angel watched as the Centauri concentrated. She felt nothing. What was Zema thinking?

Suddenly, a sharp pain invaded her skull.

"Stop!" she yelled, grabbing her head.

Zema ceased immediately. "It is the crystal. It has done something unusual to the female's brain."

"Is it serious?" Yondel asked.

"I do not know at this time. Her brain may be developing beyond our capabilities. I should not have hurt her."

"Hey, what do you mean?" The pain in her head ceased. Besides, Angel didn't like being left out of a conversation that involved her. Especially since she was sitting right there.

Zema looked at Angel. "Your species uses your brain differently than we do. Parts of your brain have been altered by the crystal. We know not how or why. When I began my probe, you felt pain. This should not have happened. When we met you in 2025, I was chosen to probe you. I did not hurt you at that time."

"What was the reason then?"

"To determine your temperament."

Angel began to feel like their guinea pig. Suddenly she wanted to escape.

"You've given me more questions than answers. This crystal," she said, bringing it out from under her tunic, "has done something to my brain, but you don't know how or what. And then, to top it off, you can't tell me how I'm supposed to defeat Ahriman. That seems to me to be the main reason I'm here, I might say. What am I supposed to think?"

Yondel rose, walked around the table to Angel, and faced her. "We are deeply sorry for the damage we've caused to your world. We know not how to remedy it. We only hope that, if you can somehow discover the reason for Ahriman's evil behavior, we can fix our mistakes. He should not have been capable of such evil. None of our race is."

Zema joined Yondel. "Please, help us learn the truth. We cannot help you defeat Ahriman. You are developing enhanced abilities that are better than our own. You may be able to get near enough to discern the reasons for his evil. You may learn what we cannot."

"Please help us," Yondel begged.

"This is all we ask," Zema said, her arms spread wide.

"Yes, this is my life you're gambling with." Angel began to feel angry. *How dare they?*

"It is your decision," Yondel said.

"We will not force you," Zema said.

"Please, think of your planet before deciding," Yondel added.

"You want me to fix your problem." Angel rose and left the vicinity of the table. "I've never been more disappointed in my life." She moved toward the entrance. "I'm leaving." She took two steps and stopped. She turned and faced the Centauri, feeling guilty at deserting them. "I can't. You are the last of your kind. I'm your last hope. I cannot turn away. I don't know why I feel this way, or how I'll accomplish this task you set before me, but I'll do as you ask."

Both aliens bowed low.

"We thank you," said Yondel.

"You possess a strong sense of self-preservation," said Zema. "Your entire species does—stronger than ours. It is one reason we wanted to help you. This ability will aid you. Believe in yourself, Angel."

Angel turned to go but retraced her steps. "You confirmed my suspicions that Queen Kalika was one of you. Why don't you join her and the elves now?"

"We cannot," said Yondel. "No one in this time knows Kalika's secret. Not even the elves."

"What? They are part Centauri. How can they not know?"

"The first true elves decided that in order to blend in with the rest of humanity," Zema answered, "their origins must be forgotten. Today, the Elfin Nation believes their queen is special, that she is destined to take them to a higher level of existence someday. Kalika can tell you her story if she so desires. We will not."

"That brings another thought to my mind," Angel said. "Is it true the human race developed dwarf characteristics by breeding with your working class?"

Zema smiled. "Yes. They took a few humans underground to save them."

"Just as Kalika took a few to save, also," Yondel added.

"There is one more thing," Angel said. "If I get the job done, can you send me back to my own time?"

"No."

"We cannot."

"Please explain why."

Zema looked sad. "It was a one-way trip, Angel. We are the last. We have not the life force left to do the job. We would if we could."

"You have to accept this time as your own now," Yondel added.

"I was afraid of that from our previous talks." She hung her head and thought a moment, feeling somewhat different. Realizing why, she caught the eyes of each Centauri. "I feel the strength you've imparted to me to do this thing. Thank you. It was needed. This is my time now." Angel chuckled, her humor surfacing. "Another good reason for me to defeat Ahriman. I guess I'd better get started. The sooner this task is accomplished, the better all our lives will become."

"Our life force goes with you," the Centauri said in unison.

Angel walked to the entrance and turned to face them once more. "I will do my best to save my world. Thank you for the information you've imparted to me. I have a battle to go to." She bowed and left.

CHAPTER 12

The Chase

THE JOURNEY OUT OF THE cave into the sunshine was over sooner than she had thought it would be. Standing on the ledge that extended from the cave entrance, she looked out. The height no longer frightened her. What had happened to her in there? She felt more confident; there was definitely a subtle difference in her being. *Did the Centauri impart that to me? Maybe it happened when Zema probed my mind. If so, it's a gift I will never forget.*

Angel looked around. *Where is Avery? Why isn't he here to meet me?* With nothing else to do, she started up. As she climbed, she noticed that she could not "hear" her comrades. A half hour later, she knew why.

The camp was in shambles. A battle had been fought while she was away. Two bodies lay facedown nearby. Their clothes identified them as Ahriman's men. So, where were the others? She closed her eyes and concentrated on them. She barely sensed a familiar presence north of where she stood. She located her pack and filled it with what provisions she found undamaged. After a short search, she found her quarterstaff, thankfully also undamaged.

Angel began walking toward the presence. The feeling became stronger until she recognized it as belonging to Barak.

She found him a short time later. He was in such agony, she instinctively blocked his thoughts from her mind. She bandaged his wounds—mostly stabs—and gave him some medicine from her own pack that should ease his pain.

Roused from her ministrations, Barak held up his head. "Ahriman's men ambushed us. Took all but Serylda and myself. Find her. And the others." He lay back down, delirious from his pain.

Angel let his thoughts flood her brain. His pain had eased, thanks to the medicine. *Good,* she thought. *He's more comfortable.* Angel closed his mind from her.

"Wait. That was too easy," she said aloud. *When did I get the ability to turn others' thoughts off and on?*

She couldn't worry about that now. Barak needed a fire. She gathered the wood into two piles. After making sure Barak was still comfortable, she lit one pile. He woke long enough for her to tell him of the extra wood nearby and that she was on her way to find Serylda. He nodded and fell asleep before she stood up.

Angel looked to the north. She sensed Serylda a little westward from due north and not too far away. She found the dwarf sleeping, hidden under some brush, about a half hour's walk from Barak. Alarmed, Angel noticed a good amount of blood pooled under her head.

Serylda awoke at Angel's touch and smiled. "Angel, you're alive! Thank the Maker." She tried to rise and fell back, holding her head. "I'm so weak. Ahriman's army attacked us. I don't know how many of us survived. I had gone to the brush for a moment when they overran us. I couldn't do a thing. All my weapons were at camp. I got hit by a stray rock."

Angel checked the dwarf's head injury. "Barak is still alive. He's injured, and he's sleeping about a half hour's walk from here."

After Angel cleaned and bandaged Serylda's injury, they made their way back to Barak. He hadn't moved since Angel left him.

"When did the battle happen?"

Serylda sat next to her brother. "I'm guessing two days ago."

"We have time to rest, then," Angel said. "We cannot hope to catch them, especially in the shape Barak's in. And I'd like to see how your head is in the morning." Angel stood. "Get some sleep, my friend. We have a long trek to begin tomorrow."

Angel thought on the latest trouble. She noticed she couldn't hear Niedra. Was the cat okay? She learned from Serylda's mind the dwarves saw it run off after the battle. They weren't ready to tell her. Angel let it go.

She decided tomorrow would make the difference. It was a different world for Angel. It was her world now, and Ahriman had just walked over her friends. He had a lot to answer for. She would make sure he did … but, not tonight.

——⁓⁓⁓—————

The next morning Angel checked the dwarves' injuries. Serylda still suffered some swelling from the rock that had hit her. Other than that, she was fine. She informed Angel she knew of an herb that would help her with her headache.

Barak was definitely worse off. Along with numerous stab wounds, he had suffered a very deep gash on his upper right arm that had incapacitated it. It was his fighting arm. He'd be out of commission for quite some time. With a little help, it could be saved. But it meant they'd need to find someone to take him to Jasper and soon.

"Leave me here," Barak told them. "I'll be in good enough shape to move in a few days. Then, I'll make my way to Jasper and follow you from there with more men." He sat up, and with Angel's help, leaned against a nearby tree. "You need to follow them. Learn where they're heading. I can't help you in any fight. But I can go for reinforcements. Serylda knows how to leave a dwarf trail. We will find your path. So, go."

Angel squatted beside him, not sure he was able to do what he wanted. He appeared too pale. Her conscience told her he was too weak to be left alone.

"He's right, Angel," Serylda agreed. "We have to leave him here. He will do all right."

"I can't leave him here to die."

Barak grasped her arm and squeezed. She felt strength in that grip that surprised her.

"I don't intend to die, Angel. I'm a dwarf. We are stronger than you think. More than this is needed to kill me."

"Okay, my stubborn friend." Angel relented. She rose and smiled down at him. "But, no one is invincible. Not even you. I'll let you have your way, even though it's against my better judgment."

"Thank you."

"There is one thing I'd like cleared up. Why haven't you made a fuss about Serylda coming with me into danger?"

"We now know for certain you are the Alastrine Savior. Since Serylda has proven herself time and again, she has earned the privilege to do as she wishes. I may not like it, but it is the dwarven way."

"Thank you, brother," Serylda said quietly. She placed her left hand upon Angel's shoulder. "It's time for us to go. He'll be fine. His dwarven spirit is unstoppable. I believe in him, and so should you."

"I agree." Angel turned slowly and faced the north. "And I believe our quarry is north and heading for Attor. I can feel Avery's mind in that direction."

"Okay, wait," Barak interrupted. "You will explain that before leaving. Did the Ancient Ones do something to you to allow this new ability?"

Angel turned and studied the faces of the dwarves and decided to tell them the truth. She sat down and motioned Serylda to do the same. They trained their eyes upon her. She drew a deep breath and let it out slowly before she began. She pulled the crystal from her tunic and showed it to them.

"This crystal was given to me at Krikor by Queen Kalika. The Ancient Ones brought it with them. Since I've been in contact with this crystal, I've acquired the ability to read thoughts and emotions. It was quite unnerving the first time it happened. Don't worry; I cannot harm you with this ability. And I realize your thoughts are a very private part of yourselves. I do not pay attention to them." She smiled. "I have to take that back. Sorry, Barak. When you tested me with the staff and I gave you that bloody nose, I knew what you were fixing to do. I felt so ashamed at using that knowledge that I am careful to never do that again. But that is my only transgression. Forgive me."

He grinned at her and nodded his acceptance.

"Remember, Serylda, I told you I had to keep a secret from you?"

At Serylda's nod, Angel continued. "This was it. When Queen Kalika handed it to me, she warned me to keep it secret, even from Avery, her own son. She said Ahriman may be able to use it against me; she wasn't sure how. But to be safe, I was charged to let no one know of it. And now you know."

Barak coughed. "You have known what we think for how long now?"

"Since a week after Niedra joined us."

"Did anyone else know of this?"

"Only Avery. I needed his help with it shortly before Stormy found us. I thought I was going insane." Angel sighed. "Anyway, Avery couldn't help me. He told me I had to work this out on my own. And that I should do as Queen Kalika had said. I couldn't tell anyone. But, now I'm glad you two know."

"You probably should not have told us," Serylda said.

"I agree," Barak added. "However, we are truly grateful you trusted us with this information, Angel. Now, you two must go. If you can read my thoughts, you know how determined I am about this."

"Yes," Angel agreed. She took hold of his hand and tried to give him relief from his pain. "I wish you luck, my dear friend, in reaching Jasper. We shall see you at Attor with help in your wake." She let go of his hand, feeling his pain ease a little.

"Thank you, Angel." Barak nodded. "I felt the help you imparted to me. I am very grateful. Now, go."

Angel retrieved her pack and weapon. She dug out some more medicine and handed it to Barak, and then she and Serylda left him and headed toward the canyon. Serylda's things still lay somewhere in the camp. After they retrieved most of her possessions undamaged, they headed north. Serylda set the pace.

Angel wondered how many of the squad still survived. *How is Avery?* She barely felt his presence. How much longer would Stormy allow them to live?

"Are you reading my mind?" Serylda asked an hour later.

"No," Angel chuckled. "I've been concentrating on Avery."

"Can he sense you?"

She closed her eyes and concentrated. "I don't think so ..."

"Can you sense Barak?"

"Very faintly. He's fine. I hope he stays where he is for at least two more days. He needs the rest."

"How about any others of the squad, especially Telek?"

Angel opened her eyes and smiled. "No, sorry. They're too far away. I think the only reason I can sense Avery is that, being an elf, he can broadcast to me."

"Thank you, Angel."

Silence settled over them once more. Seeing the camp in shambles had made Angel realize how important she was to these people.

Ahriman needed to be reckoned with. She had to do what she could to rid this world of him and his kind.

Wait. What caused me to feel this way? Do I really want to risk my young life on such a hopeless task? Funny, she didn't really feel it was hopeless. So many counted on her. She didn't feel the fear she had harbored in the mountains. *Did the Ancient Ones do something to me while I was in their company to release me from my fear?* That thought brought a question to her mind.

"Serylda, how long was I in the canyon?"

Serylda stopped long enough to dig up a root near their trail. "You were gone two days and nights." After brushing the dirt off the tuber, she took a bite. Seeing Angel's questioning look, she said, "Medicine."

Continuing on, Angel nodded her understanding. "Two days, huh? It didn't seem that long. Thanks."

What happened to the time in there? The Centauri hadn't talked that much. What had they done? Had she been unconscious for a time?

Well, whatever happened, it was in the past. She didn't care. All that was on her mind was the rescue of Avery and her comrades. She loved the elf, and he was in the hands of Ahriman. That foretold danger for her. If Ahriman found out about the crystal from Avery, she'd be dead. And Avery would never forgive himself. She knew of his love for her, too. Determination quickened her step.

"Hey," Serylda said, panting. "Slow down!"

"Sorry." She waited for the dwarf to catch up to her. "It's getting dark."

Serylda leaned against her staff to catch her breath. "What do you want to do?"

Angel scrutinized the dwarf. "You need rest, my friend. Do we stop?"

"I can go until midnight. But, please, at a slower pace. We can be closer to our target that way."

Angel gently probed Serylda's mind, barely touching it. Her stamina was amazing. "Okay, my friend. Until midnight. Then you need rest. No argument from you either."

Though they didn't know at the time, when they stopped for the night, the girls had traveled twenty-seven miles, quite a feat considering that one of them was suffering with injuries. Angel wished she had a map. She needed to know what lay ahead. She'd ask Serylda in the morning. They ate a meal of jerky, dried fruit, and water. Leaning against a tree, Angel noticed the dwarf was having trouble breathing. Her breaths were coming in gasps.

"Are you okay?" Angel asked alarmed.

"Yes. I'm just tired. Really. I need a little rest and I'll be fine." Serylda took a bite of the root she carried, lay down, and closed her eyes. "Please, don't worry about my breathing. It's a form of respiration known to aid in healing. I'm sorry I alarmed you." She fell asleep in moments.

Angel watched the dwarf sleep for a little while, just to reassure herself. Serylda snored her usual way. So, Angel relaxed and decided she should get some rest also. They hadn't been worried about anything coming upon them; they slept under a rather dense bush, one that hid them well.

Just before sunrise something brought Angel instantly awake. It felt familiar yet dangerous. She realized a second later that it was a badgercat. But not Niedra. Another female cat with babies was about to discover them.

Gently using her ability, Angel probed the female and gave it a false trail to follow. Safer for it and them. She quietly woke Serylda and motioned her to follow silently.

"Badgercat," Angel mouthed. Serylda's eyebrows disappeared into her bangs. She nodded and followed Angel away from the danger. Angel grabbed their packs and weapons on the way out.

"I had hoped it was Niedra," she said quietly.

Serylda laid a sympathetic hand on Angel's. "I wish I could help."

"Since we are up, are you ready to resume our trek? Or do you need more rest?"

"I'm fine. The medicine I used yesterday has worked its magic. I saved enough for today. By nightfall, I should be healed."

"By any chance, do you have a map? I'd sure like to look at one right now. If not, can you tell me how far we've traveled and how far we have to go before we reach Attor?"

"As a matter of fact, I do have one. Barak gave it to me before we left Krikor." She dug in her pack still talking. "Barak taught me how to read one years ago. Here it is." She spread it on the ground and studied it a moment. "We gained nearly thirty miles yesterday. At our present speed, we should be able to do the same, perhaps more. I can move more easily now, and I have more stamina than I did yesterday."

"Where would that put us? How close to Attor?"

Serylda pointed. "Here."

"How long will it take for us to reach this lake?" Angel pointed out what to her was the Great Salt Lake. *No telling what it's called now,* she thought.

Serylda pondered the question. "I'd figure maybe nineteen days."

"And we'll be three days behind Ahriman's men the whole way. We'd better get going."

Halfway through their second day, Angel sensed another badgercat. This time it was friendly. She stopped in her tracks, and her cat, Niedra, appeared from the bushes behind them. Angel gave the animal a big hug.

"I'm glad Niedra is fine," Serylda said.

"It's such a relief." Angel sat back next to the cat. "But I think I have a job for her. I don't know how she'll react. Serylda, I plan to send her to Barak to lend him a hand."

"It would be a test for both of them, I think." Serylda chuckled.

Angel projected the idea to the cat. Niedra thought a moment and agreed to Angel's proposal.

I think Black One okay with me. He let me help.

Thank you.

You be okay? You not need me?

Not right now, my friend. Barak needs you more. Find us at Attor.

I go now. Be safe, Angel.

You too, Niedra.

And the badgercat gave a screech and leapt back the way they had come.

"Amazing," Angel said aloud.

"What?"

"Niedra used my name. She's never done that before. Her use of our language is becoming stronger."

Their days consisted of traveling from the crack of dawn to midnight. They stopped when necessity demanded, and they ate twice daily. They didn't set a watch during the night; they could hide easily enough and thought the time would be better served in sleep.

The days turned into weeks. The race to Attor took its toll on Angel. She had to catch the enemy troops who held Avery before they reached Attor. She felt fear when she thought what Avery's mind harbored about her. Still, she started slowing down while the dwarf sped up. Serylda was healed and became more indifferent. Angel sensed a blood-revenge growing inside her friend. Serylda became more aggressive the closer they got to Attor. Angel was thankful to be a friend of the dwarf and not her enemy.

On a day that Angel reckoned to be around August 4, the third week of their trek, the girls came across a farm. Angel's senses screamed danger. "Careful," she whispered.

The dwarf raised her left arm in acknowledgment. They readied their weapons and, very cautiously, checked for the danger Angel sensed in the barn.

Once inside the barn, Angel nearly lost her nerve. With her hand held against her mouth, she walked the length of the barn. The girls found the mutilated remains of two horses and several chickens. There was even a housecat.

Who could be so sadistic? The sight threatened to turn her stomach. She felt Serylda harden her resolve. She followed the dwarf's example and did the same. Leaving the barn and the carnage inside, they emerged back into the sunshine.

The house stood quietly in front of them. As they neared, she motioned Serylda to take the rear of the structure. The dwarf nodded and disappeared around the corner. She crept to the front door and pressed her back against the side of the house. Closing her eyes, she concentrated on sensing anything inside. *Nothing. So far, so good.* She sensed Serylda's readiness in back and decided it was time to enter.

Her heart pounded as she crept forward. She tried the latch. Not locked. She pushed the door open. She brought up her staff in readiness. Still nothing. Not even a sound, except that her heart was beating so loudly she felt sure Serylda could hear it from the rear of the house.

She took a deep breath and entered the building. *Don't stop. Get away from the door,* she admonished herself, realizing she stood in the line of fire. She moved out of the doorway and into the shadows.

Then … she heard footsteps. She brought her staff to readiness.

"Angel?"

She released her breath in one long sigh. Serylda, of course. But, why hadn't she sensed the dwarf before she said her name? *Did my own fear block my senses?* It didn't matter at the moment. No one was home. They didn't even find a body. A relief to Angel. She didn't think she could have stood to see a human being mutilated like the animals in the barn.

"Stormy must have taken the owners hostage," Serylda said.

"I'd rather think they weren't home when Ahriman's army came through. I believe that's who did that horror in the barn." Angel shuddered. "Why would anyone torture any living thing, especially like that?"

"Your guess is as good as mine, friend. They'd just better not do that to our men."

Angel's stomach gave a loud rumble. "I guess I'm hungry even after seeing that carnage in the barn." She led the way into the kitchen. "Let's see if there's anything to eat in here."

"Good idea. I'm hungry, too."

"I know," Angel said, then stopped. "Oops, sorry. I'm trying very hard not to read you. I guess I feel so comfortable around you, I didn't think before opening my mouth," she confessed. Her ability had returned with the disappearance of her fear. She had to remember that.

Serylda smiled. "Don't worry, friend. I trust you implicitly. I'm not mad." They began their search of the kitchen. "I want Ahriman to pay for the evil he's caused," said Serylda. "And the only way that will be accomplished is to get you to his stronghold in Attor."

Serylda found some onions under the sink while Angel found a sack of flour in a cupboard. Other than that, no more food was to be found.

"I could make this into a dumpling stew," Angel suggested.

"Sounds good," Serylda agreed. "I'll try to round up some meat. Maybe I can find some other vegetables to go with it."

"Just don't go into the barn for the meat."

"No. That is too grizzly, even for me," Serylda said. She walked out the back door.

Angel tried to forget where she was and went to work on the onions. Her mouth was actually watering. She chuckled at herself. She hated onions. She must really be hungry. What would Stormy say about that?

Stormy. Strange that she thought of her twin as Stormy now. When did that happen? *Oh, sis,* she thought. *What happened to you? Why are you so evil now? The torturing, the killing? What kind of hold does Ahriman have on you?*

A tear slid down her cheek, and not from the onions. She went back to her work, chopping the onions and making the dumplings.

Serylda returned with a freshly killed rabbit and potatoes and radishes she had found. She cut the dressed rabbit and added it to the bubbling stew while Angel did the vegetables. An hour later, their stomachs full, they retired to the living room.

"Do you think we'll catch them?" Angel asked. She leaned back on the couch and closed her eyes. She was so tired, and the couch was so soft.

"If we keep pushing ourselves, I believe we can." Serylda stretched until her bones popped. "We should catch up to them near the Salt Lake about four days from now." Suddenly, she bolted upright and stared at Angel.

Angel was startled. "What?" She had felt nothing from the dwarf before her sudden movement. *Why? What happened to my ability to sense Serylda? I'm not frightened. In fact, I'm pretty relaxed at the present.*

"How would you feel toward me if I had to kill your sister? That objective may come up."

"Good question." She thought on it. "I don't know, Serylda. I know she's killed ... that she's turned evil. But, I also feel Ahriman is controlling her. If that is so, she may not be responsible for her actions." Angel sighed deeply. "I just hope we find the answer before something happens we both will regret later."

"I agree, friend. For both our sakes." Serylda rose and lay on the mattress they had brought in from one of the bedrooms. "I guess we should sleep now. Daylight is only a few hours away."

Angel agreed and joined her on the mattress. Perhaps her tiredness was keeping her from reading the dwarf this time. *Sounds as good an excuse as any other,* was her last thought before sleep overtook her.

———— ⁓⁓∘◟◝◜◞◝◜◞∘⁓⁓ ————

Someone shook her.

"Go away." She moaned and turned over.

"Angel, it's time to rise. We need to get on our way."

Oh, yeah. This is not a dream. It's real. Too bad. She opened her eyes and sat up. "Those few hours sure went by fast. I could use another two."

Serylda grinned her agreement. She rose and headed for the kitchen. Angel stretched and followed. The girls ate a breakfast of cold stew. It wasn't all that good, but it filled the empty spots, giving them the energy they needed for their march to Attor.

On the way out the door, Serylda informed her that the Salt Lake was located about ninety miles farther north—three days' march if they pushed themselves to travel thirty miles a day, no easy task in the high terrain that faced them. Angel nodded. They kept to themselves all morning, saving their strength for the rush north.

That afternoon they came upon an abandoned campsite. According to Serylda, it had been used two nights previously. It felt a safe enough place for a quick nap. Angel relied on the dwarf's sense of time to wake them at nightfall.

When Serylda woke her this time, she rose immediately. Although she was still tired, her body felt better for the rest.

Pushing themselves, they traveled forty miles that day.

The next afternoon found the girls in sight of their goal. In the far distance, from their vantage point in the mountains, Angel made out the faint shores of the Salt Lake. And that evening they chanced upon another campsite. This one proved to be fresher; it had been used the night before. Their quarry lay a short distance ahead of them.

"Ahriman's men camped here last night," Serylda voiced, her words agreeing with Angel's deduction. "We made good time. We are closer than I figured we could get."

"I agree. But I feel we both need rest. We're nearly too exhausted to fight, if need be."

"We can sleep until daylight. Our quarry won't be too far ahead even so." Serylda pointed to a rather impenetrable looking group of bushes. "That appears dense enough to hide us. Do you sense any danger, Angel?"

"No. I think we can sleep safely."

But Angel had lied to her friend. She hadn't been able to perceive anything since the night at the farm. She wondered if she'd lost her gift … if she'd lost control. She didn't know how or why the loss had occurred, and it frightened her. She had become used to it, depended upon it. She should tell the dwarf. It was wrong not to, since Serylda was her protector and friend. But Serylda showed so much confidence in her, she feared what the dwarf would think. Angel couldn't take that away from her dear friend.

Angel surveyed her surroundings. The city that stood on the east side of the lake was gone. She observed no intact buildings, just rubble with a few girders showing against the sky. The war must have wiped out the great city. There had been such a beautiful temple near the center of town. It was a shame it was gone. In her past life she'd had several friends who were Mormons … great, caring people.

When Serylda suggested they rest in the brush, she gladly approved. It would be a disaster if they were caught this late in the chase. They moved into the dense growth and made a temporary camp. They ate a cold supper of berries Serylda had found on the trail earlier in the day; a fire would be easily seen from their position. Both girls fell asleep as soon as their heads touched ground.

That night, Angel dreamed of the fateful day she and Alison— Stormy—had left the designated trail of Carlsbad Caverns, changing forever all they had known. She awoke when, in her dream, she found herself back in Jasper, on the floor, regaining consciousness under the watchful eyes of hundreds of dwarves. She returned to sleep, realizing it had only been an hour since they'd gone to sleep.

An hour before daybreak, they found themselves back on the trail. The Salt Lake disappeared from their view when they moved lower into the valley. After the scene Angel had observed that had shown her the absence of the great city, she feared for her life and Serylda's. What if there was residual radioactivity in their vicinity? Were they safe from that? Only a Geiger counter could tell them.

At high noon, Angel held up a hand. She sensed danger. *Good,* she thought. *At least my gift hasn't deserted me entirely.* The danger came from just ahead. She pointed. A plume of smoke trailed into the clouds a few miles in the distance. Their quarry lay directly in their path. They had caught up!

The girls resumed their trek, only more cautiously. It had taken them twenty-one arduous and hungry days to hike nearly five hundred miles. Angel hoped it had been worth it.

Closer now, they left their exposed position in the road. Angel sensed their foes strongly. She was thankful she hadn't mentioned the lapse in her ability to Serylda. Suddenly, Angel stopped and pulled Serylda down into the brush with her. Serylda looked at her questioningly.

Her voice barely above a whisper, Angel said, "I want to see if I can reach Avery. Let him know we are near."

Serylda nodded and watched as Angel closed her eyes in concentration.

Angel thought hard on the man who had captured her heart. She opened her eyes and stared at the group ahead and out of sight of the girls. She ignored everything around her but the task she set for herself.

Avery, do you hear me?

She felt a tingle in her mind.

Avery. Hear me, please. Are you there?

Angel?

She barely made out his mental voice. *Yes! Serylda and I are nearby.*

Barak?

He went for help. He was too injured to come with us. How are you? Are you hurt?

Nothing.

Avery?

The tingle and his voice were gone. She'd lost contact. She turned toward Serylda.

"Well?" the dwarf mouthed.

Angel shrugged, and whispered, "I had him for a few seconds. Then he was gone. I don't know how I lost contact. I didn't get a chance to ask him if he was hurt, or how many of our friends still live."

"Was he killed?"

"Doesn't feel that way. Perhaps he just passed out." Suddenly Angel gasped and clutched at her breast.

"What!" Serylda grabbed her arm, seeing the pain.

"Something awful just happened." Angel glanced around and stood. "Come. We need a closer look."

Very cautiously they crept ahead, staying mostly in the brush. The going became impossible. They chanced the road and kept close to the vegetation. Still, their quarry stayed out of sight. Angel had misjudged the distance. Their quarry was farther away than she thought.

Two hours later they chanced upon a campfire, still warm. The Salt Lake lay off to their west, and Attor was north. Their quarry was heading for the geysers and sulfurous fumes of that dreaded place. Angel thought how sad that the Yellowstone of her time—a beautiful, unique place—had become the stronghold of such evil.

Serylda called out, unmindful someone may hear. Her voice was unusually cold and hard. Angel joined her near a group of bushes. Serylda pointed and then bent down and pulled a body from under the shrub. Both girls gasped when they realized the identity of the body. It was Javas, his head nearly severed from his body.

"Ahriman will pay dearly for this," Serylda said. Her voice carried no emotion, only steely determination. "I swear a dwarf oath I will make him pay."

"You loved Javas."

"Yes, Angel. We were to marry this fall. It was to be a special occasion to unite the Dwarven and Elfin Nations."

Angel felt deep sympathy for her friend. She looked back the way they had come, then forward toward their destination.

"Ahriman has a lot to pay for. He took my sister and turned her into something evil. Because of his influence, she has killed. She killed Evrak. And now Javas is dead, your mate and my friend." Determination filled Angel's face. "Yes, Ahriman will pay dearly for his evil."

Serylda stared at Angel for a few seconds. "I want you to know I will kill Stormy if I get the chance. I blame her. She is in control of Ahriman's army. I am sorry she is your sister. But I care not."

Angel placed her hand upon the dwarf's arm. "I can't condone what you want to do. Alison, or rather Stormy, is still my sister. I have to rescue her from Ahriman. I won't stand in your way, my friend. But," she lowered her hand, "I won't help either."

"We have an understanding. You take care of Ahriman. He is yours. Your sister is mine. But be warned, once a dwarf makes an oath, nothing stands in the way. I may accidentally kill you if you interfere. Please, I do not want that to happen."

"I know. I feel it in you. But, as I said before, I will not help kill her. I plan to try to save her. She deserves that." Angel held up a hand to stop Serylda's reply. "Even so, I will not get in your way. I have promised."

Angel hardened her heart and stabbed her quarterstaff against the ground. "You are right. Ahriman does have a lot to answer for. He is mine. He took my sister from me and killed our friends and their family members. I don't yet know how, but I will defeat him." She glanced back the way they had come, seeing back to her past. She whispered, ". . . or die trying."

Taking a deep breath, Angel said, "C'mon. We're getting nowhere like this. We have to follow them and get inside Attor."

They started walking, trailing Stormy and her army. The girls didn't talk. Angel felt rage build inside herself and tried quelling it. She needed to stay calm. When she had regained her control, she felt Serylda's rage. It proved to be stronger than her own. Once again, she was thankful the dwarf was her friend. Serylda would make a formidable foe.

Angel understood something important inside herself. When she controlled her own emotions, she heard others' emotions. She had to be master of her mind. Did the Ancient Ones know of this? Or was this something new to this time? She was unique and carried a crystal no one else did. Another thought occurred to her. *Is this a way to defeat Ahriman?*

And defeat him she would. This was her new home now. And he wasn't welcome in it.

The girls hugged the greenery, staying hidden and eating berries and other edible vegetation Serylda found. They filled their water skins at every opportunity. They slept without fires to keep from being detected.

Ten days later, they caught their first sight of the stronghold of Attor. They looked on as Stormy marched her prisoners in and the gate closed.

"Well," said a disgruntled Serylda, "what do we do now? How are we supposed to get inside that?"

That afternoon they crouched behind one of the few bushes in a devastated landscape. It gave the impression of a battlefield minus the bodies.

Angel studied the castle for a few minutes. She turned to Serylda and rose. In a quiet but determined voice, she said, "I'm going to walk up and knock on his door."

CHAPTER 13

Barak

BARAK WATCHED THE GIRLS DISAPPEAR from his sight. He wondered if Angel knew how much she had helped him when she eased his pain. He shifted to be more comfortable. The wound on his arm began oozing, and he attended to it. Angel's ministrations began to wear off. He retrieved the packet of herbs Angel had left with him and rummaged through the packet looking for a particular herb. The bark of a willow tree contained the medicine to ease his pain. If only she had left some.

Thankfully finding a chunk, he broke a tiny piece off and placed it in his mouth. He had not the energy to boil water and prepare it in the correct fashion. This expedient way would work, though the taste left much to be desired. His only worry was that it might force him to sleep. He decided to not worry about that because his pain had returned with a vengeance. Retying the bandage as best he could using his teeth, he managed to stop the oozing blood. After that task was accomplished, he spit out what remained of the bark in his mouth and lay down. His last conscious thought was a hope that a badgercat wouldn't show up while he was in his weakened state.

Time passed. He dreamed about Niedra. He was back in time on the day he and his men met up with the three badgercats. They stood, weapons ready, as the cats advanced upon them. Barak proved the lucky one, to a point. He was farthest away when the animals attacked. But also, he was the only one without a weapon. He berated himself for leaving his ax near the fire that burned beyond where his men were suffering the attack. A moment later, it became worse. A fourth badgercat arrived. Its coloring was a little different than that of the others, more orange in color. He looked into its iridescent orange eyes. It studied Barak and backed him into some brush. Then, it did an unusual thing. It turned and guarded him. Why would it do that? What was this animal who appeared to be protecting him? The cat growled and …

Something awakened him. He looked up only to be staring into the eyes of his dream. His heart skipped a beat. *This is how it will end?* He wouldn't give up without a fight, even if it was with his fists.

The badgercat sat back on its haunches and Barak's eyebrows rose. *Why would the cat do that?* He wondered.

"Niedra?"

The cat mewed back.

Fascinating. Angel must have something to do with this.

"Well, we may not be able to talk to each other, but I bet I know how you came to be here. Angel sent you, didn't she?"

The cat mewed.

"Well, I'm still not able to travel, my feline companion. I need a little more rest. Now that I have you to watch over me, I feel safer. Thank you."

The cat mewed once more and turned away. She found a place a little distance away from Barak and sat in a guarding position. He lay back and relaxed. Funny, his dream had turned into reality.

Sleep once again overtook him. It was the fourth day since the girls had left him.

When he awoke the next day, the cat was nowhere to be seen. It must have been all delirium on his part. He could only be thankful no other badgercat had found him while he was unconscious. As that thought crossed his mind, Niedra padded up and laid some form of tuber at his feet before sitting back on her haunches. They stared at each other a moment; Barak was astonished at seeing the animal again. It hadn't been a dream. The silly cat was here.

He took advantage of the help she awarded him. The tuber turned out to be a type of potato, full of energy. Though it was covered in cat saliva, he was hungry. He wiped it as best he could and took a bite of the raw tuber. It had a strange but not unlikable taste. *Probably from the cat.* After eating most of it, he felt some of his energy return.

"Well, my feline companion, are you ready to help me reach my home?"

She mewed and rose. Stepping next to him, she allowed him to climb up on her. Unable to straddle the cat, he just hung across her back. She began to slowly walk toward Jasper and help.

Sometime during the day, he woke up and realized he'd fallen into unconsciousness. He still lay across the big animal's back, but he felt tired and sore. Sensing his discomfort, the cat stopped. He climbed off and stood.

"Thank you, friend. From this day forward, I shall look upon your kind differently."

She mewed.

He studied the terrain. They weren't making good progress, but at least the cat had traveled in the right direction. What he needed was a dwarf scout to find him. He knew he couldn't send the cat to do that. She'd only get herself killed. How would Angel feel about him if he let that happen?

After another thirty minutes they resumed their arduous journey. A dwarf lying across a giant badgercat traveling east at a slow pace. What a sight they made.

In fact, a dwarf scout had seen them and observed the spectacle before deciding to check it out. After he came within thirty yards of the two, he recognized Barak.

"Sire?" he yelled at a safe distance.

Barak looked up and fell off the cat. She reached down and gave him a lick to check make sure he was okay. With her help, he stood and looked toward the voice.

"Who's out there?"

"It is Carver Greenstone, sire. Are you okay? Is that a badgercat?"

"Yes, Carver. She won't hurt you, believe it or not. She is Angel's cat. We cannot harm her in any way, understand?"

"Yes, sire." Carver moved to be near the two. "What would you like me to do, sire?"

"How far are we to Jasper?"

"Oh, about three days' hard march. I can get help if you choose me to do so, but, sire, I have misgivings leaving you alone with that." He pointed to the badgercat.

"Go and rally the army. Tell Dwarflord Ganesh that Angel has traveled to Attor along with Serylda. Have them meet me on the way."

"Yes, sire. I will leave immediately." Carver turned and started away. At Barak's voice, he turned back.

"Tell my sire Devlak is with the elves. They are to meet us there."

Carver bowed and left.

"Well, my friend, we've been found by my kinsman. We are saved."

Three hours later, Niedra stopped. Barak saw her fur bristle. He surmised they were in trouble, but from what he didn't know. Suddenly he realized his greatest fear. Two badgercats appeared from around a bush ahead of them. He stood stock still as Niedra padded up to them. He watched as she slapped both on their noses and drew blood. They bent low in deference to her and left.

The time went by slowly for Barak after that. No badgercat stood in their way as they slowly marched east. Barak's strength slowly returned, and he needed Niedra just for support until he found a suitable walking stick. Five days later, the dwarf army with Dwarflord Ganesh in the lead found him. The physicians patched his wounds and provided additional medicine, and the army began the long march to Attor. Niedra stayed at Barak's side. He wasn't sure who was protecting whom.

Halfway there they merged with the elfin army led by none other than King Iomar and Queen Kalika. Just behind them, Devlak and the rest of the squad, healed of their injuries, followed. Happy to be reunited with his comrades, Barak introduced everyone to Niedra. She became the combined armies' mascot. Queen Kalika was able, in a small way, to convey Niedra's thoughts to all.

"Niedra," the queen said, "is thankful we do not harbor hatred toward her. She feels this to be the beginning of a peace between her kind and us. She carries the designation of mascot with pride."

The combined army cheered as Niedra rose on her haunches and gave a great battle cry. The march to Attor and the coming battle once more began.

———⁓⁓⦿⊙⦿⊙⦿⊙⦿⊙⦿⊙⦿⊙⦿~~———

Serylda watched with fear for her friend as Angel "knocked on the front door." *That is one headstrong human,* she thought. *There are some in the Dwarven Nation that Angel could put to shame.* And Angel had happened to become Serylda's dearest and best friend. In her heart, Serylda prayed Angel would find a way to save her sister. Being a dwarf and swearing a blood oath made it difficult for her to feel sympathy for Stormy. Perhaps that was another aspect of their friendship—the ability to see the good in all living things.

Serylda had a hard time spotting Angel because of the distance. She watched as someone raised the portcullis. Several armed guards exited and surrounded Angel. After watching them escort her inside and lower the gate, Serylda turned. She decided to meet up with the army. It did her no good to wait here. She'd mull over Angel's predicament and perhaps do something foolish.

In the distance she noticed dust in the air. The army was fairly near to her. Suddenly, she met with two badgercats. Their noses appeared newly healed—from a fight, she surmised. Knowing what her brother had told her of these animals, she readied her staff. If she was lucky, she could fend them off with few injuries long enough for the army to reach her.

They circled her warily, watching her every move. Serylda realized she may not survive, but determination clouded her emotions. The battle maid was ready.

Then, out of the bushes rang a sound Serylda would never forget. Niedra sprang from nowhere and tore the nearest cat in half. The other cat snarled at Niedra, and then both badgercats circled each other and ignored Serylda. Slowly she backed away from the confrontation. She could not help Niedra; she'd only get in the cat's way.

From nearby she saw the army rushing toward her. An arrow whistled past her and through the feral badgercat just as she spotted King Iomar emerging from the mass of dwarves and elves. His bow was empty of the arrow that now lay embedded in the stray cat. Niedra padded up to Serylda and licked her hand.

"Thank you." She petted the orange fur. "I will always be in your debt."

The cat mewed.

"King Iomar," Serylda bowed. "I am so glad to see you. I may be a dwarf, but when confronted with not one, but two badgercats intent on killing me, any help is very much appreciated."

"My friend and ally, your father would not forgive me if I'd done anything less." He turned as Dwarflord Ganesh emerged from the crowd.

"I've heard a great deal about your exploits, my daughter," the dwarflord said as he hugged her. "I aptly named you, it seems."

Queen Kalika joined them. "It is time for us to resume our march to Attor."

With agreements heard all around, Serylda led the army to its destination. They arrived a short time later. Dwarves and elves worked to set up tents and light fires as they made ready for the wait. Nothing could be done for now. It was up to Angel, behind the massive walls of Attor, to decide their fate. The combined army began their long wait.

CHAPTER 14

Attor

ANGEL TOOK UP HER QUARTERSTAFF and headed for the front entrance of the castle. It stood in the distance. Geysers of steaming water spouted, and hot mud boiled in patches that lay between her and her goal. The air reeked strongly of sulfur. The stench permeated everything. The whole area appeared a disaster. It hadn't been this bad in her time. The entire valley appeared desolate. Living things had grown here and walked this land two thousand years ago. Had the supervolcano exploded? No, the lake was still present. So, what had happened? *Perhaps another thing Ahriman has ruined*, she decided.

Taking her mind off the devastation, she thought back to the conversation with Serylda a few moments ago. "Are you crazy?" Serylda had grabbed Angel's arm when she'd announced she'd just march up to the door and knock. "They'll just put you into the dungeon and forget about you. They know you are meant to defeat Ahriman."

"I don't believe they'll do that." She'd been amazingly calm. "He wants to meet me. Remember, his consort is my sister. He knows who I am and why I'm here." She shook her head. "No. They won't put me in the dungeon.

Angel had smiled and gently removed the dwarf's hand from her arm. "Don't worry, Serylda. I'm more worried for you than me. He won't kill me. Anyway, I sense others coming from the east and south. The elfin and dwarven armies are near. You must stay and greet them. Prepare them for what is about to happen." Then she'd given Serylda a big hug and released her. "We shall see each other soon. Take care, my dear friend."

———

Returning to the present, Angel's heart beat faster and louder the closer her feet carried her to the entrance. She admitted to herself she was terrified. She stood outside the moat and looked up. Above in the parapets, men guarding the front gate stared down at her. Her knees threatened to give out beneath her.

"Steady, girl," she said aloud. "Where's your courage? You can do this. They won't kill you. They would have already if they were going to."

She took a deep breath. Her body shook, giving away her fear. Where had her courage gone? It had stayed with Serylda, that's where.

A foul smell coming from the moat encircling the castle greeted her nostrils. Was it poisoned, or worse? She felt heat emanating from it, too.

Aloud, she said, "Ahriman. I've come to challenge you. Open your gate and face me. That is, if you aren't a coward."

"Bold words from such a small being," a voice drifted down to her.

The drawbridge lowered over the moat. A dozen men rushed out and surrounded her. One took her staff and threw it in the moat. Tragically, she watched her gift boil away as the men laughed. *A very acidic fluid.* She was glad they hadn't thrown her in!

The men took her inside. As they approached the main building, a grand door opened. Stormy stood on the threshold, the evil aura stronger than Angel remembered.

"Welcome, sis. We wondered how long it would take you to arrive. Ahriman has been expecting you." She dismissed the guards who obediently returned to their duties. "You'll soon see we aren't the demons everyone makes us out to be." She led the way through the foyer to stairs that rose through the castle tower. No railings stood between them and the drop below as they climbed.

"If he's not evil, why did you kill for him?"

Stormy laughed. "That was a necessity. You'll understand once you meet him. You'll see."

"I will never understand how you can be so cold-blooded about taking another's life. You are no longer my sister. I have no sister."

Stormy chuckled. "You're being a little dramatic, don't you think? Just like when we were kids." They stopped at a landing and faced a door.

"I do not think so." Angel hardened her heart. "My sister's name was Alison. You are Stormy. So, I repeat, I have no sister."

Stormy laughed. She produced a set of keys and unlocked the door. She pushed Angel inside.

"Now, I suggest you relax. Ahriman will send for you shortly. I'll send you something to eat and drink in the meantime. I bet you're hungry." Very lightly, she touched Angel's face. "Don't worry, sis. Everything will turn out fine. You'll see." She turned and left, locking the door behind her.

Now what? She was inside the castle. But she was a prisoner nonetheless. She could do nothing but worry. How could she not? She had just marched up to an enemy's stronghold and demanded entrance. Could she have been any more stupid? Serylda had tried to keep her safe until help arrived. Angel had told her the armies were near. But, no, she had to go anyway.

She knew why. She wanted a look at Stormy before Serylda got hold of her. The aura still lingered. What could she do to save her sister? Yes, they were still sisters no matter what she told Stormy. She had an obligation to try to save her before Serylda had Stormy in her sights.

Angel studied the room. It was lavishly decorated in red. One corner sported a four-poster bed adorned with blood-red, gilt-edged pillows. Elaborate carvings covered the posts. Angel moved closer to see and backed away. Dragons stared out at her. A fireplace took up half of one wall. A couch festooned with more of the same red pillows faced the fireplace. The furniture matched the dark-red, shaggy rug situated in the center of the room. The room's only window boasted curtains to correspond.

Angel placed her head in her hands. The redness of the room gave her a headache … perhaps the intent for the décor. Her hands trembled with nervousness. Another reason for the décor … to unnerve whomever they deposited in there. A noise from the other side of the door startled her and made her jump.

Two guards entered with swords drawn. A stooped, old man stepped between the guards. He set a tray on a table near the couch. He gave her a toothless smile and left. The guards backed out and relocked the door.

Stormy had kept her word and had sent her food and drink. The tray held a variety of fruits and vegetables along with several types of cheese. Two goblets shared the tray. She sampled the one containing a red liquid. It tasted like wine, but with a strange and unpleasant twang. The other goblet held water. She tried it. It tasted very bitter. She wasn't hungry after all, she decided. The food and drinks were more likely drugged. She wasn't falling for that trap.

She walked over to the window. Pulling aside the curtain, she looked out. She could see over the outer wall and out to the area where her friends waited. The desolation lay before her and freedom. She caught a glimpse of movement out on the field of campfires and embraced the comfort she felt.

She calmed her mind and felt the terror that inhabited the castle. It grew stronger. She closed her mind to it.

Strange. It took this frightening experience to teach herself how to accomplish the ability to close off alien minds from her own. At least her own terror didn't cause her ability to falter. She must have accidentally learned the trick when she thought her own emotions closed her mind. She hugged the thought to herself, giving herself comfort.

She wondered if she could keep control when she was brought before Ahriman. *Will he turn my ability against me?* He was one of the Centauri. The Ancient Ones had kept her from recognizing the passage of time. They also told her he could sense them. *Will he be able to sense my gift? After all, the crystal I possess came from his world.*

Darkness fell and still she had heard nothing since food had been brought to her. *How long ago was that? Where is Ahriman? Is he making me wait to soften me up? To grate on my nerves?*

A noise at the door. Stormy entered, breaking into her musings. She turned to see two guards, swords drawn, enter next. The time had finally come. Angel left the vicinity of the window and approached them, not allowing them to see her apprehension.

"I'm sorry for the delay, sis." Stormy walked to the couch and took a seat. The guards stayed by the doorway. "Ahriman is so busy these days. He sent me to keep you company."

Angel said nothing. She returned to the window and looked out into the gloom.

"I hope you enjoy my room. Bet you didn't know that. Ahriman gave me this room. It used to be his. He let me decorate it how I liked." Stormy kept chattering as Angel ignored her.

The night was proving tiring to Angel. Stormy, when she was Alison, could talk all night about nothing in particular. She hadn't changed in that respect. Perhaps in time, Stormy would tire of talking to herself and leave. Angel decided she'd test how long her sister could keep up her sermonizing. She went on about how good Ahriman was to her. Angel just stood at the window and said nothing.

A half hour went by and Stormy rose. "Fine. Be that way." She joined the guards at the door. "I thought you might like some company. Since you are ignoring my questions, I guess I'll leave." She ordered one of the guards to take the tray. "I hope you sleep well, sis. See you tomorrow." Laughing, she left, followed by the guards. Angel heard the door lock behind them.

Alone again. It would be a long night. She glared at the bed. *No telling what has happened beneath those sheets.* Well, she could lie upon them and not under them. It was a warm night, and she needed the rest. *No use debating the issue,* she thought. She lay down on top of the covers and fell asleep almost immediately.

Something aroused her from deep sleep. Someone was in the room with her. No, two people slithered nearby. She heard their voices. Opening her mind, Angel felt utter terror from the castle. That wouldn't do. She moaned and shut her mind to the horror.

"Shush," said one of the intruders.

"She's only dreaming," said the second, a little louder. "It's the drug. She's still asleep."

"Okay. If you ain't scared, you check her for anything," whispered the first.

"Not me," said the second. "This was your idea. You check her."

"Not so loud, you dope," said the first.

"You're the one who's a dope," said the second. "You're stupid and scared."

Angel heard both men approach her. Time to end this little charade. She moaned louder and stirred. Tossing some more, she began to rise.

The intruders beat a hasty retreat and slammed the door. She walked to the door and checked it. Yes, they had left it unlocked. She grinned. *A great advantage for me!*

She opened the door and peeked out. No one in sight. She was alone. She left the room. Finding the key still in the lock, she locked the door and pocketed the key. Looking up, she spied a landing as far above her as the foyer was below her. She started to climb. She knew what lay below. What was above?

She reached the landing about five minutes later, panting. In front of her stood a door. Where it led she had to find out. She turned and looked back the way she had come. It was a very long drop to the foyer. She didn't relish a slip here. At least she no longer harbored a fear of heights. No one stirred below. She was safe, for the time being.

She tried the door. Not locked. She opened her mind to the room beyond. Nothing. She opened the door and stepped inside. Her heart beat so strongly she was afraid it would burst. No one greeted her. She relaxed and checked out her surroundings.

This room was as black as the other one was red. Black walls, black furniture, black curtains. She inched her way to the window and pushed the curtain aside. The room faced the same direction as the red room.

The crystal around her throat began to heat up, warning her of danger. Looking down, she gasped. A man wearing long, black, flowing robes entered the tower with Stormy by his side. Her crystal grew hot, and Angel knew that man was Ahriman. She began to panic. Bile rose in her throat at her terror. She sensed her mind closing down from her fear. Time stood still for her. She had to move and retreat back to the red room. She rushed to the door in the hopes she could get back to the hated red room, but it was too late. Ahriman and Stormy had just passed its door.

Angel was trapped. She had no choice but to reenter the black room. She closed her eyes to the inevitable, and forced herself to calm down. The time had come to confront Ahriman, whether she wanted it or not.

The door opened.

Stormy entered first.

"Well, well, well," she greeted Angel. "I think I need to punish some guards. No matter." She chuckled. "Ahriman, I'd like you to meet my sister, Angela. Of course, everyone here believes she is the Alastrine Savior and here to defeat you. She believes we are sisters no longer."

"I've heard a lot about you, my dear," he said. His voice carried a deep timbre with silky soft overtones. "I have been impatiently waiting to meet you. And now, my wait is over. Here you stand before me." He laughed softly and moved over to the black couch sitting near the window. "Please, Angela. Won't you join me?" He patted the space next to him.

Curiously, she felt a need to do as he said. Slowly, she moved toward him. But something wouldn't let her go. Something burned upon her chest.

The crystal! She had momentarily forgotten about it in her panic. She stopped in her tracks. Could he sense her mind on it?

"I don't want to sit down just now," she whispered.

"But I so want you to join me." His determination became too strong to ignore. "Come here and sit," he demanded.

Her head began to hurt. She felt his mind trying to manipulate hers. *So. Is that how he's controlling Alison? And if that's the case, how am I to defend against that?*

"I said *come!*"

This time she heard the command aloud as well as inside her mind. His thoughts proved stronger than her will. Her heart pounding, she obeyed and sat beside him. His vileness washed over her, and she cringed inside. The crystal burned her chest.

The burning sensation of the crystal gave her the power to regain her mind. She accomplished it without Ahriman realizing she did so. Somehow the crystal was telling her something. If only Ahriman would stop his probing of her mind. She allowed him to see only what he wanted to keep him in the dark, but it proved tiring to her.

"And now, my dear," he was saying. "What is this I hear about you wanting to kill me? Can you tell me how you'll accomplish this impossible feat?"

"I don't know how," she intoned. "I was just told to do it."

"I know, my dear. I read your mind on the matter." He rose and stood at the window, looking out. "Stormy, please take her back to her room. I'll talk with her later. You may stay with her if you so desire."

"Yes, my love." Stormy walked to Angel and pulled her to her feet. The girls left, accompanied by the sound of Ahriman's evil laughter.

"See?" Stormy asked. "He's not bad. You can see why I love him, I hope."

"No," Angel remarked. "He's manipulating you, and you cannot see it."

"I don't believe you. I'll prove it. Instead of staying and talking to you, I'll get Avery to keep you company. You'll see. He's fine and has been treated well." Stormy smiled as she pushed Angel back into the red room. "I'll be back shortly, sis." She closed the door and locked it.

Back again in the red room, Angel sighed, hating the place even more. She sat down on the couch and thought over the strange meeting with Ahriman. It hadn't been as bad as she had feared. The crystal had helped her keep her sanity, and Ahriman hadn't caught on.

She had learned one fact from the mind contact that would shock Ahriman if he found out she knew. He wasn't as sure of himself as he let others believe. He was more afraid of her than she was of him. She found courage she never knew she had with that information.

Angel leaned back and closed her eyes to the exhausting redness of the room.

She had another dilemma to think about. What was her crystal trying to tell her? It had quit burning as soon as she'd left Ahriman's vicinity, as soon as the girls had left the room. Her answer to the defeat of Ahriman lay in this unique crystal from another planet. *If Stormy does as she promised and brings Avery to me, perhaps he can help me.*

Several hours later, the door opened and brought her to focused awareness. She looked up to see Stormy smiling from the doorway. Guards shoved a disheveled Avery inside, and Stormy left, relocking the door.

Angel ran to Avery. He pulled her close.

"Oh, my Angel." His voice held disapproval. "I thought you safe. Why are you here?"

"You forget my destiny," she said as she gently left his arms. "I'm supposed to defeat Ahriman."

They sat together on the red couch.

"I believe he's too powerful now, Angel. You should have stayed away. He'll hurt you, maybe even kill you, unless we join him."

Suddenly Angel felt manipulated. She probed Avery's mind gently and felt nothing. Then she saw the aura around him, very subtle. Ahriman was using Avery just as he was using her sister. She would get no help from him. In fact, she couldn't say anything about the crystal. It would reveal her secret to Ahriman. A tear slid down her cheek.

"I'm sorry, Avery," she consoled him. "I thought I could save the world. Everybody kept telling me I could. To the point that I believed them."

He pulled her close. "Don't worry, my love. We'll survive no matter what."

To herself she thought, *I have to find the way alone, my dearest elf. You cannot help me any more than the Ancient Ones could.*

Aloud she said, "Even if we don't, we have each other now." She looked into his eyes, seeing only blankness mirrored there. With her heart breaking, she could only smile at him.

He smiled back. The door opened.

"Time's up, Angel," Stormy said upon entering. Two guards followed her in and moved toward Avery. They escorted him out. Stormy laughed when Angel rose. "Oh, I only meant time's up for your reunion. Ahriman will see you again tomorrow. He said try to get some sleep. You won't be having supper." She spread her arms wide and chuckled once. "Sorry." She turned and left, again locking Angel in the hated red room.

Time to figure things out, Angel said to herself. She pulled out the crystal, exposing it to the evil of the place. It was the key. It had helped her keep control of her own mind when Ahriman probed her. It had enabled her to reveal what she wanted to disclose to Ahriman and not what he wanted her to give away. He thought she had succumbed to his will like the others around her had done. She hadn't, and he never knew that.

She replaced the crystal with a thought forming in her mind. Maybe that was the answer. The crystal had enabled her to see the hesitation in his mind. Perhaps if she were to open himself to his faults, he would turn against himself. That sounded well and good. But it would have to wait until the next time she confronted the Centauri.

She took Stormy's advice and went to sleep. No one disturbed her that night, and she slept soundly. She relied on the crystal to warn her if she needed awakening.

The next morning, unusually refreshed, she awoke to Stormy entering the room. Without speaking, she led Angel back to the black room. Ahriman was absent. He would arrive after eating his breakfast, Stormy told her. "Which you don't get. Chew on that as you wait." And she left the room, slamming the door shut and locking it.

And chew over her predicament Angel did. She understood Ahriman's reasoning for making her wait. He was trying to wear her down. He must have felt something blocking his attempt to control her. Probably why he made her miss a few meals. She believed now even more that the crystal was the answer to defeating this monster.

Ignoring Queen Kalika's advice, she pulled the crystal from its hiding place. It was time to show it to the world.

At that precise moment Ahriman entered the room.

"I hope you are ready for me," he said. "I plan to teach you a few things about myself, maybe about yourself, too."

Angel turned to face him. "I'm more ready than you think, Ahriman." She held up the crystal to his eyes.

He laughed. "You think that bauble will save you?" He pushed her down onto the black couch. "I've known about that stone for some time now. It came from my planet. Yes, I know you are aware I'm Centauri. And I read about the stone from your precious Avery's mind."

She began to fear him. Had she made a mistake? She had done what Queen Kalika had told her not to do. Well, it was too late. The damage was done. The only thing to do was try the crystal on Ahriman the way she thought to do last night.

She concentrated on Ahriman, tried to probe his mind. A duality met her attempt. One entity felt stronger and had control of the mind that was Ahriman.

He laughed again. "What are you trying to do? I sense your mind touching mine. But it will do you no good. I am stronger than you. I've been doing this for centuries now." He broke her mental contact and savagely pushed his mind into hers.

Angel moaned. He hurt her. She closed her eyes and concentrated with all her being on the crystal. Unconsciously, she took hold of the stone in her left hand as she did so. She found the strength to push him away.

"Excellent!" he said, nonplussed. He regained control of her mind in a more gentle fashion. She began to accept his control, hearing his words inside her mind.

Yes, you could become my consort and replace your sister beside me. Rule with me, Angel. I can teach you many things. Your mental powers aren't fully developed yet. I can help you with that. Let me do so. He held out his hand to her.

She took it. The crystal became a vague memory. The pain in her head subsided.

"Yes," he whispered. He chuckled and sat down beside her. "Leave us, Stormy."

Stormy did as she was told.

"And now that we are alone," he began, "I can start your training. I know you sense my control over your sister—"

No! Something screamed inside her head. From somewhere deep, she knew that, if she allowed him to do what he planned, all would be lost. She would lose her sense of self despite the crystal.

"Please, stop," she begged.

"Why?" he laughed. "You want this. And I will have you as my own. I will triumph over you and all the others."

The crystal burned her. It would not be ignored.

Ahriman looked at the thing hanging around her neck. "But first, you must get rid of that necklace. Throw it out the window."

She took hold of the crystal. At that moment, she broke free of his mental hold of her. She realized she had regained control without him realizing it! She had to outfox him. Let him think he still controlled her.

"I can't let it go," she told him.

He pushed deeper into her mind, hurting her. She allowed him. "You must let it go," he demanded.

She turned toward him, tears streaming down her face. "I can't."

He took hold of her hand as it grasped the crystal and attempted to pry her fingers free. That was her opportunity. She saw through him and knew his secret. She used her other hand and held his in a tight grip.

The evil residing in him was not Centauri. Sometime in his past, Ahriman had been captured and possessed by an enemy known to the Centauri. The enemy now suppressed the owner of the body. Its plan was to fool everyone until the time was right. Her task became clear. With her help, the Centauri spirit stirred deep within Ahriman from a long and terrible sleep. Now she had to help it regain control.

"I know you, Ahriman. Or whoever you are," she said. "You are Centauri but you are also another. The Other does not belong here."

She turned the crystal to physically contact his palm, and once more tightened the grip. "Please, Centauri. Wake up and regain the control you once lost."

"*No!*" Ahriman backed away and broke contact with Angel. "I have control. I will prevail. The Centauri will die."

"If he does, so do you."

She felt the horrible evil emanating from the Other. It was strong. She had to be stronger. It harbored hatred for the human race. It wanted to destroy everything.

Something else sent off a warning inside her. She ignored it.

She returned to the Other, retaking hold of his hand. It had to die. With her control over the crystal, she was able to go deeper into Ahriman's mind. She found the Centauri. It wallowed in despair and shame at the things that had happened in his name.

No! she thought at him. *It's not your fault. Hear me. Take hold of me. I will help you.*

Something shoved her away, again causing her to break contact. It was Stormy.

"You're killing him! Stop!"

"He is evil, Stormy!" She shoved Stormy aside and regained her hold on Ahriman. Angel focused on Ahriman. "You do not belong in here," she addressed the Other. "Begone!" She brought the crystal back in touch with Ahriman's skin for emphasis. "Leave this Centauri in peace. *Now!*"

"*No!*" cried Stormy and Ahriman at the same instant.

Anguish filled the voices of both Ahriman and Stormy. The Centauri crumpled to the floor, bringing Angel with him.

Stormy stumbled once and fled the room.

"Thank you," whispered the Centauri. His voice was different, softer and at peace. "The entity has left me." He sighed. "I am sorry for the evil I've caused on your planet. Now, because of you, I can die with dignity. Tell my people you prevailed." He closed his eyes and quietly left the living. His body dissolved into thin air. No trace of Ahriman endured.

In the Great Crack, the Centauri standing along the wall stirred and drew a sigh of relief. The deed had been done. Ahriman had been set free. The Centauri's enemy, who had captured their beloved leader's son without their knowledge, had possessed him and caused such damage, had been wrenched from Ahriman's body. The moment Angel realized what had controlled him, Yondel and Zema knew the reason for Ahriman's evil. Their faith in their race once again grew strong. A heavy burden fell from their shoulders.

They now had a job to do. Each in turn walked up to the Centauri at the wall and kissed them, imparting the knowledge they'd just received. When they reached the last of the four, another appeared. Ahriman had joined his kind on the wall. Every Centauri on Earth smiled in gratitude at that moment in time.

CHAPTER 15

A New Beginning

Angel closed her eyes and allowed the tears to fall. Ahriman had meant no harm. It had been an alien entity who had caused all the evil. How ironic it was that it took a member of her race to save another race. She knew the Ancient Ones would rejoice in the fact that Ahriman had been a Centauri at heart at the very end. His soul had returned to the ways of his people.

But what happened to Alison? The next order of business was to find her. She had acted strangely when the alien entity left Ahriman. Angel walked out of the room into the hallway. The guards wandered aimlessly throughout the castle. No one knew of Alison's whereabouts, though Angel asked every being she came across.

She ordered a handful of the wandering guards to open the gate and lower the drawbridge. Once that task was accomplished, she ordered two others to fetch the dwarf and elf armies. As they left to do her bidding, she spied a handful of guards disappearing, Stormy among them. It was too late to follow. She needed to get to the dungeon and let the imprisoned people out.

She found twenty people and Avery in the dungeon. All of them hugged her as they left. Avery was the last to be set free. Arm in arm, Avery and Angel walked up from the lower levels to meet the armies in the sun outside the gate.

Once outside in the fresh air, Angel told Avery what had transpired between her and Ahriman.

"That seems too easy." Avery shook his head. "I fear he will be back."

"I don't see how. I watched him die."

"No, Angel," Avery corrected her. "The evil still exists. It will return. But don't despair. You did what you were supposed to do. You defeated the evil."

"But if I didn't destroy it, where did it go?"

"You said you saw Stormy flee shortly afterward?" he asked. "I deem it fled inside her."

"Oh, Avery," Angel closed her eyes. "I can't live if she turns into the monster Ahriman was. I sensed something in him that sent a warning throughout my being. It frightened me."

The armies rode up and broke her train of thought. Angel felt relief that the armies weren't needed. In the lead she spied her trusty animal friend. Niedra bounded toward Angel with such happiness that all who watched the reunion were alarmed. That is, until they saw Angel's face. She caught the big cat and didn't want to let go.

"I'm sure glad to see you, my dearest." The cat growled in agreement.

"She found me and helped me," Barak said, ambling up to them. "I'll tell you one thing, Angel. She gave me one big scare running into me when she did. She showed her happiness in finding me by bringing me a few tubers to eat that day." He hugged Angel before continuing. "Because of her, Angel, the dwarven people will look differently upon badgercats. No longer will we try to eradicate them."

"Thank you, Barak"—Angel grinned—"from both of us." The cat growled and they laughed.

Queen Kalika pushed her way through the crowd. "Angel."

"My queen," she said and bowed.

"You have done what you were destined to do. We thank you."

"But, I feel I've failed. The evil still exists."

"Yes. Your sister may no longer be a part of you. I am sorry for that. But you defeated the evil in Ahriman and set him free. He is at peace. The Ancient Ones thank you for giving them back their faith. As do I," she said, with a twinkle in her eye.

"You sensed when he died." Angel said that as fact.

"Yes. All Centauri did."

"Then you know of his last words."

"Yes. I would consider it an honor if you would tell the people his last words."

Angel turned to the crowd and addressed them.

"Ahriman was sorry for the evil he caused. I am here now to tell you it wasn't his fault. You see, he had been possessed by an evil entity … an evil spirit, if you will. I was able to cast this spirit out of him, and he quietly died. He was one of the Ancient Ones. They are a race of beings, as you know in your history, who came to help us. They are a very peaceful race that had a hard time understanding how the evil existed. Now we can be at peace too."

Serylda pushed her way through the crowd. "Where is Stormy?"

Angel sensed the unsatisfied revenge in her friend. "She fled with a few guards. I don't know where. I am sorry."

"You remember my oath."

"Yes, Serylda. I do remember, and I understand."

"Good." Serylda smiled and gave Angel a dwarf hug she'd never forget. "I'm glad you're alive."

Angel hugged her back. "Me too, dear friend. Me too." She felt glad her sister was far away from Serylda's revenge.

Another thought entered Angel's mind as she released Serylda. "I don't see Cornellius here. What happened to him?"

According to King Iomar, Cornellius is still looking for his bird," Barak replied.

A dwarf detached himself from the crowd. Angel looked over and bowed. "Dwarflord Ganesh."

The dwarflord bowed back. "For accomplishing your task, I name you Dwarf Friend now and forever, with all the privileges that go with it."

She raised her eyebrows in surprise. She couldn't help but tease him a little. "Even though I dragged your two sons and only daughter with me into peril?"

"Yes," he said, and grinned at her.

She bowed low. "I am honored, sire."

He pulled a quarterstaff from behind his back. "This was my personal ceremonial staff. Serylda informed me she trained you on one."

"Well, yes, sir. But I never got the chance to fight with the one she made me." She glanced at Serylda. "They threw it into the moat."

"I give you this in return for your work in bringing back peace." Dwarflord Ganesh handed her the weapon with a bow to her. "May you never have to fight with it." She accepted it with humility.

"It is fortunate you did not fight and take a life," said King Iomar, stepping forward and joining his consort. "You were still innocent in that respect when you confronted Ahriman. That helped you defeat the evil."

"Yes," the queen agreed.

"And that is what helped me see the evil from the good in Ahriman, right?" Angel asked.

"Yes." Queen Kalika motioned someone forward. "We have a gift for you, as well. Do you remember Ariel?"

Angel nodded. "She's your personal servant."

"Now, she is yours."

"I'm sorry? I don't know if I can accept this. I never had a servant before. I believe in equality among all." She faced the girl. "Meaning no disrespect to you or the queen, but I don't really need a personal servant."

"But you will if you are to be the next queen of the Elfin Nation."

The crowd turned deathly quiet. Angel turned back to the queen, not believing her ears. "Please explain that statement, my queen."

"I may be queen now. But you will be queen after me."

"How is that possible? I'm not elfin."

"Have you looked at yourself lately?" Serylda interrupted.

"No, why?"

"You are developing exquisite elfin ears and brows, my dear," Avery said behind her.

"How is that possible?"

"I believe the crystal has done more than give you the ability to hear thoughts," Queen Kalika contemplated.

Avery smiled. "And if you marry me, you'll have no choice, since I'm next in line to become king."

Angel spun around. "Marry you?" She smiled slowly. "Oh, Avery, I will marry you!" She flung her arms around him. Laughter and cheers surrounded them.

She let Avery go. "Serylda? Where are you?"

"Right here, friend," she said behind Angel.

"Will you be my maid of honor?"

"I'd be more than happy to."

Angel made a sweep of her hands. "I was afraid and unhappy when I first found myself here and realized what everyone wanted me to do. But you all have given me friendship and a home I'm proud to call mine. I don't deserve this happiness." She allowed one hand to fall to her side while the other rested gently on her breast. "I am extremely honored."

"We are the ones who are honored by your presence," Dwarflord Ganesh said. "In fact, I should apologize to you."

Angel frowned. "Whatever for?"

"I treated your sister and you as spies when Barak found you wandering in our home."

"Well, I wasn't too friendly myself. So don't hog all the remorse, sir."

"Well," Avery interrupted. He took hold of Angel's hand. "I, for one, am glad it's over. Let's set up camp and rest for the night. We have a long trek ahead of us."

Everyone agreed and set about erecting tents and lighting fires. No one wanted to sleep inside Attor. In fact, the dwarven army smashed it to rubble that evening. It would stand as a testimony to anyone who thought to rule the world.

Angel hoped that was a lesson well learned. She joined the elves, smiling and feeling glad to be alive.